Love's Madness

He pulled her up sharply against him, and his hand clapped over her mouth in a way that was rough. "Are you mad!" he hissed. "Coming out here at night like this!"

She didn't notice the way he spoke. Instead, she held very still. And waited. When she didn't move, didn't try to answer, didn't try to escape, he slowly lifted his hand from Rebecca's mouth.

When she still didn't speak, he gave a sigh of exasperation. And held her close against him as she rested her head against his chest.

"Please don't be angry with me," she said. "I noticed you out here, and I had to come down. I thought, I hoped, you would be happy to see me."

With a groan he bent forward and rested his forehead against hers. Rebecca moved her hand from his sleeve to stroke the side of his face. He turned and kissed her palm.

"Something is troubling you," she said softly. "What is it? What are you afraid of?" she asked.

"You."

The
Reluctant
Thief

by

April Kihlstrom

A SIGNET BOOK

SIGNET
Published by the Penguin Group
Penguin Putnam Inc., 375 Hudson Street,
New York, New York 10014, U.S.A.
Penguin Books Ltd, 27 Wrights Lane,
London W8 5TZ, England
Penguin Books Australia Ltd,
Ringwood, Victoria, Australia
Penguin Books Canada Ltd, 10 Alcorn Avenue,
Toronto, Ontario, Canada M4V 3B2
Penguin Books (N.Z.) Ltd, 182–190 Wairau Road,
Auckland 10, New Zealand

Penguin Books Ltd, Registered Offices:
Harmondsworth, Middlesex, England

First published by Signet, an imprint of Dutton Signet,
a member of Penguin Putnam Inc.

First Printing, March 1998
10 9 8 7 6 5 4 3 2 1

Prologue

"A street thief?" Hugh Rowland asked, quirking an eyebrow upward. "You want me to pretend to be a street thief? How, er, unusual. Why?"

Sir Geoffrey Parker looked at the young man before him and tried to imagine him in the stated role. Sitting as they were in his elegantly appointed study, both men dressed exquisitely in evening attire, it was impossible. And yet, Sir Parker knew it could be done. That was precisely why he had chosen Rowland.

"First," he said, handing Rowland a glass of brandy, "tell me, are you betrothed? Or likely to become betrothed any time soon?"

Mystified, Rowland shook his head. He took a sip of brandy and there was an edge to his voice as he explained, "There was a time when I thought I would. But I am long past such foolishness. I doubt I shall ever marry. I am a younger son and my brother has both a wife and several sons in his nursery, so I may please myself. And I have no desire to make some woman unhappy by shackling her to my person, when I have no patience for such things."

"An interesting way of looking at it," Sir Parker said mildly, leaning back in his chair. "I shan't ask you why you feel that way. All I care is that the men I use have no such entanglements in their lives. I thought you did not, but I wished to be certain."

"You may rest easy on that head. I am not now, nor do I expect ever to become betrothed," Rowland repeated.

Sir Parker nodded. He took a sip of his own brandy and chose his words carefully.

"I need you, Rowland, because there is a ring of thieves preying upon members of the *ton*. They have been remarkably successful. What makes them unique is that they are run by a group of men whom we believe to belong to the *ton* themselves. They supply the necessary information, and the ring of street thieves does the actual stealing. Both sides profit."

Rowland frowned and leaned forward. "Why not let me try to join the group of gentlemen?"

Sir Parker stared into the fireplace and his expression was impassive as he replied, "No, we've some men already attempting to do so. But we believe they don't hear everything that goes on. We think it is headed by Lord Halifax."

Rowland started and Sir Parker nodded grimly. "Just so. We think Halifax does not tell the others everything he does, or has done for him. There is also a lady who is helping us, who has been able to give us some useful information. But it is still not enough. We need someone from the other end of things, someone who might be able to find out if our suspicions are true."

"Bow Street Runners?" Rowland suggested.

Parker shook his head. "We need someone who can pass as a street thief and yet understand how a member of the *ton* might think. Naturally, I thought of you."

A smile crooked up the corners of Hugh Rowland's mouth. "Naturally," he agreed. "What do we know?"

Sir Parker shook his head. "Very little. We *think* Lord Halifax may be heading up this ring. And that he has recruited young men from some of the finest families in England. That makes it sticky."

"I imagine it would," Rowland agreed. "What if one of them recognizes me?"

"That's another reason I chose you," Sir Parker said with an ambiguous smile. "You are known, by reputation, as an incorruptible man—which means you couldn't persuade them to believe you to be one of them if you tried to join as yourself. On the other hand, you have been out of the country for some time and the only men likely to know you by sight are most unlikely to be part of such a ring. Unless they are my men, of course."

"Of course."

"We think we know where they mean to target. I will give you the direction and it is up to you to figure out how to disguise yourself and how best to bring yourself to the attention of the street thieves working for this group of gentlemen. You will report back to me as often as you can and I shall do what I can to help you."

For a long moment, Hugh Rowland stared at Sir Parker. Then, lazily, he took a sip of brandy and said, "When do I begin?"

"At once." He hesitated, then looked at Rowland from beneath hooded brows. "There is one more thing I should tell you. Be very careful. There have been one or two really nasty murders this past year and I would dearly love to pin them on Halifax, if it should turn out he was responsible. If he was, he has been careful enough not to let the gentlemen he has recruited know about it. He is not going to risk scaring them off, but he wouldn't hesitate to kill you if he got wind of what you were about."

Hugh frowned. "One thing I don't understand. Why involve the other young men at all? Why not simply run this rig himself and keep all the profits?"

Sir Parker smiled a nasty smile. "Two reasons. One, I believe he gets a great deal of amusement out of corrupting young men. Second, he needs them for the information they can give him. Yes, he could probably discover it himself, simply by discreetly asking the right questions. But if he did, sooner or later someone would notice the coincidence between his questions and the robberies. This way there are others to draw the attention instead of him."

"I didn't like Halifax before," Hugh said mildly, "but I am discovering I dislike him even more than I would have thought possible."

He set down his glass and got to his feet. "If I am to begin at once, then I'd best go and arrange my affairs so that I can safely disappear, with no one the wiser or likely to ask questions about where I've gone. As for the disguise, I have something in mind already."

Sir Parker also rose to his feet. He chuckled as he said, "Somehow I thought you would."

Lady Rebecca and her twin, Lady Penelope, the youngest daughters of the Earl of Westcott, were staring out the window into the afternoon rain.

"It is so boring here!" Penelope complained. "I should much rather be back home in the country."

Rebecca sighed. Her sentiments were not so very different from her sister's. They were not identical twins, but they had been nearly inseparable from birth and in general saw things very much alike.

"Well, we are here, Penelope. We are here to catch husbands, just as our sisters did. Good husbands."

Penelope caught the note of discontent in Rebecca's voice and pounced on it.

"You haven't forgotten, have you? We made a pact. A pact that neither of us shall marry, no matter how much pressure Mama and Papa and Aunt Ariana put on us to do so."

Rebecca hesitated. "Yes, but that was some time ago. What if our sentiments change?"

Penelope shook her head impatiently. "How could they change? How could we wish to give some man power over our lives? Or hand over our fortunes to him? To someone who would have the right to treat us as little more than children, if he wished?"

Rebecca stared out the window, torn between conflicting emotions. She understood Penelope's fears, for she shared them herself. And yet a part of her dreamed of the day she would meet someone she could love and share her life with, just as her sisters had done.

Still, Penelope was her twin and desperate to hear her answer. Rebecca could not look in those eyes and tell her that it was possible she would change her mind. After all, she might not. Time enough to tell Penelope if it happened.

"Very well, we still have a pact," Rebecca said softly.

Penelope gave a tiny crow of delight. "Famous!" she said. "And you'll see. In time, Mama and Papa and Aunt Ariana will come to understand and agree."

Somehow, Rebecca did not think that likely, but she was too kind to say so aloud.

Chapter 1

If Rebecca had not been so restless that bright spring morning in London, she would never have caught herself a thief. Not that she knew he was a thief right away. That knowledge came much later.

But Rebecca was restless. She felt as though she would burst if she stayed indoors a moment longer. Surely, she decided, there could be no objection to her taking a walk about the square this morning with her abigail.

But she was not about to risk asking permission. Her abigail looked at her oddly but agreed willingly enough and, with her sister Penelope still asleep, Rebecca and her maid slipped out of the house.

Her intelligence was lively and she was consumed with curiosity about everything she saw. The maids scrubbing the front steps before anyone was likely to be out and about to see them. The servants hurrying to or from the market with the day's shopping. The boys and men who stood waiting to sweep the street ahead of anyone who wished to cross, or chase down a windblown hat, or hold the reins of a horse for a penny.

One such man in particular drew Rebecca's eyes. She had seen him before, these past few days, and there should have been nothing to set him apart from the others. Except that Rebecca thought there was an unusual degree of intelligence in his fine blue eyes. They seemed a stark contrast to the shabbiness of his clothing, the way his light brown hair looked badly in need of combing, and his evident need of a bath.

There was almost an air of kindness about him. He wielded his makeshift broom and chased windblown hats and held the reins of horses with the best of them. He peppered his words with coarse oaths Rebecca had never heard before. But he did not shove the smaller boys out of the way, as they did each other. She had even seen him help one of the smallest ones to his feet and give the boy a coin.

He was an enigma. Rebecca had never met, had never been allowed to meet, someone like him before. Now, as her steps drew her closer to the man, Rebecca realized that he looked as though he were badly in need of a good meal. He looked as though he needed someone to take care of him.

In short, Rebecca discovered that she very much wished she could take him home with her.

Just as that heretical notion occurred to her, there was a commotion on the street. Someone came running toward her. He was large and burly and carried something clutched beneath his arm. Two footmen from the house near her own were giving chase. The man with the deep blue eyes seemed to step almost deliberately into the running man's path. The burly fellow swerved to avoid the man with blue eyes and came straight toward Rebecca.

She tried to move out of the way, but she couldn't. Suddenly he was shoving past and she was falling toward the street—and into the path of an oncoming carriage.

Her last thoughts, as she fell, were that Miss Tibbles was never going to forgive her for this!

Hugh Rowland caught the blur of movement out of the corner of his eye. Cursing roundly, he ignored the man running away, and the footmen coming close behind, and grabbed instead for the person who was falling toward the street.

There was no time to pull her backward so he grabbed the woman and, holding her tightly to his chest, rolled with her across the cobblestones as fast as he could. They just barely avoided the hooves of the horses and wheels of the coach that could have crushed both of them. Then he yanked the woman to her feet and hurried her to the other side of the street, to safety.

He cursed again. At her. At himself. This was precisely the sort of thing he should not get himself involved in. It would draw precisely the wrong sort of attention to his person. And yet he didn't let her go. She seemed too shaken and far too unsteady on her feet. And then she spoke.

"Please, don't be angry with me," she said earnestly, clutching at his shirt. "I am most grateful to you for saving me."

Startled, Hugh found himself looking down into the gentlest, kindest face he had ever seen. She seemed as fragile as a feather and yet he had the impression of steel beneath the soft exterior.

For all the dirt that clung to her now, she was clearly a lady. The quality of her fair complexion and wispy curls of blonde hair escaping her bonnet would have told him as much even if her gown had not been made of a green sprigged muslin and her pelisse of a hunter green velvet that surely cost a king's ransom per yard.

Just the sort of girl he generally avoided like the plague. He wondered if it was possible she knew him, but it seemed most unlikely. He had not spent much time in London, as himself, and she looked as though she was just come out of the schoolroom herself. Besides, he thought, he could never have forgotten her!

Still, it was fortunate she was unlikely to look at him twice. Not a street vagabond such as he appeared to be.

Especially when he towered over her and would no doubt frighten her out of her wits the moment she regained them.

Even as he watched, her eyes widened as she stared up at him. But not, he realized, in fear.

"You," she breathed softly.

Rowland almost dropped her in surprise. "Me?" he croaked, in a high, squeaky voice. Then, recollecting himself, he added, forcing his voice lower and firmer and pitched only for her ears, "Wot's you mean, m'lydie? I ain't never set me glimmers on you before you landed yourself in the street t'day."

She gently pushed against his chest with her daintily gloved hands and Hugh reluctantly let her go. She was, as he had instinctively known, stronger than she first appeared, for nothing seemed to upset her. Not the interested onlookers crowding around, offering japes and jeers. Nor the fact that he towered over her.

No, she simply set her hands on her hips and looked directly into his eyes as she said, in tones as low as his, "I have been watching you."

Rowland gulped. Suddenly his collar seemed far too tight, for all that his shirt was unbuttoned at the top. He looked around at the crowd, which was growing more interested by the moment.

He had to get her out of here before she said anything more. He didn't know what she had seen, or what she meant to say, but he wasn't about to risk her calling attention to anything more about him.

Besides, she didn't belong out on the street this early in the morning. Any fool could see that. The question was, how to convince her of that.

Suddenly she seemed to make up her mind. "You are coming home with me," she said briskly.

Rowland gaped at her. "Wot, m'lydie?"

"I said, you are coming home with me. You have, with-

out a doubt, saved my life, and my father and mother and
aunt will surely wish to reward you, with at the very least
a good meal and some money, and possibly even with a
post at my aunt's house."

Hugh began shaking his head. "Oh, no, m'lydie. You
don'ts know wotcher saying."

"Oh, yes, I do," she said firmly. "Now come along. My
aunt's house is right over there."

Hugh tried to hold back, but that would have brought
him even more unwelcome attention. There seemed no
help for it. He would go, offend them by his very looks,
and be out on the street again.

Besides, he couldn't very well allow her to continue on
her way all alone, could he? Where the devil was her maid
or footman, anyway?

That last question was answered as a young woman
bustled up to them, crying out anxiously, "Oh, m'lady! I
thought you were killed for sure! It has taken ever so long
for me to get to your side, with this crowd and all."

"I am perfectly fine," the girl answered firmly. "And
we are all going back home now."

The maid eyed Rowland warily, but did not object. It
was not, after all, her place to do so. Still, her offended
expression left him with no doubt as to her feelings on the
subject.

A crinkle of amusement creased Hugh's face and he almost smiled. Perhaps he was going to enjoy this little in-
terlude, after all. He would escort the young lady home,
then leave her there and come back to his post on the
street. By that time the crowd would be gone and he could
once again be inconspicuous.

Rowland began to whistle as he followed the two
women toward the house the young lady had indicated.
He tried to remember what Sir Parker had told him about
each of the families on this street.

At the front steps, the young lady hesitated. She turned to

Hugh and said, somewhat timidly, as though afraid of offending him, "Perhaps it would be best if you went around back. Tell them you are going to be hired for a position on the staff."

In spite of himself, Rowland was amused at her presumption. What a handful she must be!

"For what post, m'lydie?" he asked with an air of innocence.

The girl blinked up at him. "What do you mean?"

"They'll want to know for wot post oi've been 'oired," Hugh said in a serious tone that was belied by the way his eyes were twinkling.

That was a facer for her; he could read it in her expression and the adorable way she scrunched up her face while she tried to think.

"I don't know," she admitted cautiously. "You aren't as handsome as the footmen Aunt Ariana usually hires. Nor would you make a matched pair with any one of them, though you are quite tall enough."

Now it was Hugh who blinked, taken aback by this frank assessment of his features. She seemed to have noticed for she smiled kindly and patted his arm as she went on, "It's nothing to be ashamed of, Aunt Ariana is simply very particular about her footmen and no one would believe she had hired you to be one of them."

Hugh made a choking sound but waited to hear what else this young lady would say. After a moment, a smile of triumph lit her face. "I have it! You shall tell them you've been hired as a jack of all trades to fix some things about the house. I know for a fact some of the door handles are coming loose."

"Door 'andles," he echoed, trying very hard not to laugh.

Somehow Rowland did not think she would appreciate his amusement and he found, somewhat to his surprise, that he wanted very much not to hurt her feelings. Be-

sides, the servant accompanying the girl was already looking at him doubtfully and he had no wish to raise her suspicions any further.

"Yes, door handles," she agreed brightly. "You can
tighten door handles, can't you?"

He tried to return to character. He stared at his feet and
mumbled, "Oi s'poses oi can."

"Good. Then let's go in. You go first, round to the back
door. And hurry, we have been standing here quite long
enough as it is. Aunt Ariana, and Mama and Papa would
be distressed with me if I drew any more attention to myself than I already have, this morning."

She stood there, patiently waiting for Hugh to do something. He found he couldn't disappoint her. Meekly, he
went to the back of the house. He would wait, he decided,
until the girl and her servant had gone inside, then he
would simply come back out front and leave. It had been
an interesting encounter, but he did have work to do.

Unfortunately, the girl seemed to have anticipated him.
When he went around to the front again, he found that instead of having gone inside, she was standing, arms
crossed over her chest, tapping her foot, waiting for him.
She was, evidently, more perceptive than he thought.

He could have gone around her and simply left, but that
would have drawn more unwelcome attention to him because he was quite certain she would try to follow. Besides, he told himself, it might be useful to make the
acquaintance of the servants in this house. Perhaps it
would, sooner or later, be to his advantage. So, once more
whistling as though he had not a care in the world, Rowland went around back. And this time he knocked.

All he had to do, he told himself, was make certain that
the family didn't want to hire him on. And once they met
him, that shouldn't be very hard to manage. He knew very
well how shabby he looked. And how badly he smelled.

Half an hour, an hour at most, and he would be out of

here and back on the street. He'd wager a great deal that the man running from the other house was part of the ring of thieves he was seeking, and he needed to find him again.

Chapter 2

Rebecca stood meekly in front of her father, hands clasped tightly behind her back. It felt very strange not to have her sister Penelope at her side to support her, but Rebecca was determined to stand up to her father anyway. She had to, for the sake of the poor man downstairs. So she stood there and didn't even flinch as her father roared at her.

"A servant? You've hired a servant?" the Earl of Westcott demanded.

"Yes, Papa."

"Why? How? What on earth could give you the notion it is your place or your right to hire a servant for your aunt's household?" the earl sputtered.

"Dearest, I am certain Rebecca meant well," Lady Westcott said, a note of bewilderment in her own voice.

"Rebecca, I am grateful that you are concerned about the welfare of my household," Lady Brisbane said mildly, "but I do wish you will answer your father's questions. It is most puzzling to all of us."

The only person in the room who did not speak, the only person in the room of whom Rebecca was at all afraid, was Miss Tibbles, her governess. In another household, she and Penelope would be considered too old to require a governess. But Lord and Lady Westcott knew their daughters far too well. Not only did Miss Tibbles remain, but she still gave them lessons every morning, Season or no Season. Now that redoubtable lady stood watching Rebecca and waiting for her answer.

Rebecca sighed. "I've told you, Papa, Mama, Aunt Ariana, the man saved my life. I thought the least I could do was to bring him back here. I thought you would *want* to reward him by giving him a position."

This last was said with deceptive meekness and a bowed head. Through her lashes, Rebecca watched carefully to gauge the effect of her words.

The earl cleared his throat. "Yes, well, of course we are *grateful*."

"Indeed, there is no question about that," Lady Westcott agreed, a tremulous note to her voice.

"But a vagabond?" the earl said doubtfully.

"He is not a vagabond!" Rebecca said hotly. "I told you. He has been earning pennies by sweeping filth from the cobblestones for people as they cross the street, or chasing down hats, or holding horses."

"As I said, a vagabond. Scarcely a step above a beggar, in my opinion. There are far too many such paltry fellows since the war was over."

"Is it their fault, Papa, that they came back from war to find there were no jobs for them?" she countered.

"Yes, well," Lady Westcott intervened hastily, "the question is what to do with this particular fellow, this streetsweep, or whatever you wish to call him. He did save Rebecca's life."

"I suppose a place could be found for him here," Lady Brisbane grudgingly acknowledged. "Though I am not certain what. Still, perhaps as you yourself suggested, simply as a fellow who is to lend a hand wherever necessary."

Lord Westcott snorted, but he did not object. It was not, after all, his house.

Rebecca smiled a blindingly grateful smile at her aunt. Lady Brisbane reached for the bell pull and a few minutes

later a shabbily dressed fellow with scraggly brown hair
and whiskers was shown into the room. His deep blue
eyes were the only feature one could distinguish beneath
all that hair.

Instantly, everyone leaned away from him and wrinkled
up their noses. It had apparently been some time since the
fellow last had a bath. If he ever had had one. And he was
large, much too large, one felt, to be standing in a lady's
drawing room.

Nor did he seem to know his proper place. He stood
straight upright, with a cockiness at odds with his situation. He ought to have been the supplicant. Instead, he
looked as if he were secretly laughing at all of them.

Rebecca was not pleased to see it. If he wasn't careful,
he was going to ruin everything! Her father was trying to
smile. Didn't the man understand what such a gesture cost
her father? How hard it was for him to be beholden to a
man who looked as this one did? Why couldn't he be
properly humble and grateful?

Rowland did understand. Perfectly. And perhaps that
was why he found himself annoyed. Still, it would not do
to burn his bridges in this household just yet. Even the
short time he had spent downstairs in the kitchens had
told him how much the staff of this house noticed. How
much comment his own hanging about the square in the
past day or so had caused. Perhaps it was time to recon-
sider his plans. Meanwhile, he waited to hear what the
Earl of Westcott had to say.

The earl cleared his throat and forced himself to nod at
Rowland. "Sir, I understand you are the reason that my
daughter is still alive. We wish to show you our gratitude
in some tangible way and therefore Lady Brisbane has decided to offer you a place in her household."

Rowland noticed the woman who was presumably Lady
Brisbane and was amused to see that she looked as if she

had swallowed a lemon. Apparently Lord Westcott thought so as well for he added hastily, "Until we remove from London, that is. Then, of course, you will become a part of my own household, in the country. If you wish it."

The woman lost her sour look and the earl appeared distinctly relieved. Rowland hesitated. He frowned. Then to everyone's patent surprise, he twisted his cap in his hands, and gruffly said, "Wot if oi'm not certain oi wants to work in this 'ere 'ousehold?"

Immediately a look of relief came across the face of everyone in the room except the young lady and the woman he assumed was her governess.

"No!" the young lady cried out.

She crossed the short distance between them and took hold of his arm. "You can't just go away! Papa, you can't let him!"

The earl cleared his throat again. "Rebecca," he said warningly, "if the fellow wants to go, we must let him." To Rowland he added, "I shall, of course, be happy to give you a reward for saving my daughter's life."

So her name was Rebecca. For a moment, Rowland wanted to refuse the reward. But that would have looked very odd indeed. Instead, he dipped his head twice, shuffled his feet again, and said, "Thank'ee kindly."

The earl reached for his purse. Lady Rebecca, however, had other ideas. She stepped between the man and her father and said again, "No! I won't let you go!"

"Rebecca!" three shocked voices cried out in reproof.

Now the plainly dressed woman in the room came forward. She stared at Rowland in such a way as to make him feel distinctly uncomfortable, for he had the impression that she saw much more than he would have liked. And then she spoke.

"Rebecca, this is not one of your stray kittens or birds or other creatures you have brought home to take care of in the past," she said sternly. "This is a human being who is quite capable of making his own choices. If you cannot be still, you will go up to your room and wait for me there."

Lady Rebecca looked as if she wanted to refuse, but she did not. Suddenly Hugh could not bear to see the look of unhappiness on her face, and he had a notion how to use matters to his advantage as well.

Before she could leave the room, he said, "Oi'd loike that job, after all, me lord. Oi could use a steady wage. S'long as oi could do most of me work outdoors. 'Andy wif me 'ands oi am, if there's work wot needs to be done."

There was a stunned silence in the room, but the look of happiness on Lady Rebecca's face, as she stood near the doorway, was enough to sustain Rowland. Yes, this might work out very well, after all. He could keep an eye on the square, hear all the latest gossip, and if he played his part right, still do what he needed, when he needed to do it.

The earl gulped visibly. He turned three shades of red, then said, nervously, "Oh. Well. Of course. Um . . . That is . . . Let me see."

One of the women took pity on the earl. She leaned forward and said to Rowland, "I am Lady Brisbane. So long as you are in this house, you are my servant and I shall pay you fifteen pounds a year. I shall also decide what work you do. For the moment I have no objection to what you propose. You don't have any other conditions, do you?"

Hugh made himself shuffle his feet, as though embarrassed to ask.

"Come, come," the earl said impatiently. "Speak up!"

Rowland twisted his hat in his hand again. "Well, um, that is, I moight need to go out, each day, for a bit. To check on me mum. She's that ill, she is."

"What?" Lady Brisbane demanded.

"Preposterous!" the earl replied.

"I don't think I have ever heard of such a thing," the other lady, presumably Lady Westcott, chimed in.

It was Lady Rebecca who hotly defended him. "How can you chide this man for wanting to take care of his mother? Of course he must be allowed time off to check on her if he needs to do so!"

Hugh had no illusions as to how the family felt. Still, they agreed. Reluctantly, but they agreed.

The moment it was settled, Lady Rebecca threw herself into her father's arms. "Oh, Papa, I adore you!" she said.

"Yes, well, there, there," the earl said, patting his daughter awkwardly on her back.

The other ladies in the room looked less pleased with the turn of events, but they said nothing aloud. Rowland strongly suspected that once they were alone together, they would enjoy a comfortable coze over the matter and happily rip his character to shreds. The thought amused him.

Now the dragon of a governess spoke. "That will be quite enough, Rebecca. You will go upstairs now, as I told you to do several minutes ago, and wait for me. We have delayed the start of your morning lessons long enough as it is."

Hugh expected her to protest but she didn't. Instead, with a warm smile directed toward him, she fairly danced out of the room. He could hear her soft steps on the stairs. Then he waited, certain the family was not yet done with him. He was right.

The moment Lady Rebecca was out of sight and the sound of her footsteps had faded, they all began to talk at once.

"You will do as you are told in this household, and no nonsense about it!"

"You will stay away from my daughter."

"Do as you are told and you will get along well enough. Don't, and you shall be out on your ear."

"Miss Tibbles, what do you think about all this?"

These last words were addressed to the dragon who had sent Lady Rebecca upstairs. And everyone stopped talking to hear her answer. It seemed to Rowland that she chose her words with the utmost care.

"I think it is as well that you hired this man to work for you. While I do not generally believe in acting so impetuously as Lady Rebecca has done today, she does have a history of bringing home stray creatures and trying to take care of them. To flout her in such attempts is to make her more stubbornly determined. I cannot help but think that close proximity to this man can only cause whatever foolishness she feels toward him to swiftly dissipate."

Rowland could not help grinning at what was clearly a slap at his appearance and character. He didn't mind. It told him that his disguise was as impenetrable as he meant it to be. Besides, he found he approved of someone watching out for the girl.

"But what if it doesn't?" Lady Brisbane asked in acid tones.

The governess raised her eyebrows in surprise. "With the round of balls and parties that have begun, and to which she is invited? Do you not think that there will be any number of attractive young gentlemen capable of giving a new direction to her thoughts?"

"Yes, of course, you must be right," Lady Westcott said slowly.

The governess nodded. "And if I am wrong, then you may attempt to banish the fellow both from Rebecca's life and her mind. But do, I pray you, try to do so without making a more romantic figure of him than he already is."

With that clincher, the family turned to the question of precisely what duties to set Rowland to, right now. In no time, he was sent off downstairs to bathe, change his clothes, and then begin his new duties, trimming hedges at the back of the house.

The last thing Rowland saw was the governess headed upstairs. No doubt to ring a peal over Lady Rebecca's head, he thought, and wished there was a way to put a spoke in her wheels. But he didn't try. Hugh Rowland was not one to go after the impossible. And a short lecture on the dangers of trusting strangers might be in order anyway to protect a young lady with more heart than common sense.

Penelope regarded her twin with awe, and more than a little doubt. "You brought him home with you? Good heavens, what did Mama and Papa have to say to that? And Aunt Ariana? Or Miss Tibbles?"

Rebecca shrugged with a nonchalance she did not feel. "They have hired him to work about the house," she said. "After all, the man saved my life."

"But a stranger? A man who sweeps filth on the streets?" Penelope persisted, all but bouncing on the bed.

Rebecca looked at her sister with wide, melting eyes. "Oh, Penelope, what difference does it make what he does in life? He saved mine! He is no less a human being for having been born in less comfortable circumstances than our own. I could not simply walk away and pretend that nothing had happened!"

"Yes, but perhaps he won't like to work in a house," Penelope suggested doubtfully. "Perhaps he prefers to be out on the street."

"Then he must learn to like it here," Rebecca answered firmly. "And I shall help him."

Penelope only shook her head. "Mama and Papa will not allow you to do so," she warned. "They will want you to have nothing to do with the fellow."

With a sense of rebellion she had never felt before, Rebecca lifted her chin, looked her twin directly in the eyes, and said, "They cannot stop me."

"Cannot stop you from what?" a stern voice demanded from the bedroom doorway.

Both twins jumped. Penelope hastily rose to her feet and blushed even though there really was nothing for *her* to blush about. She looked at her twin anxiously, but Rebecca seemed utterly at ease. She rose to her feet slowly and calmly faced the doorway.

"I said, Miss Tibbles," Rebecca replied, tilting up her chin, "that no one can stop me from trying to help someone who is deserving of my help."

"Such as your mysterious stranger," the governess retorted dryly as she advanced into the room and carefully closed the door behind her.

"Yes, such as the stranger," Rebecca said, thrusting her chin even higher.

"Very well, I shall join you in this enterprise," Miss Tibbles said. "Just tell me what you mean to do."

Whatever Rebecca expected, it was not that. She simply gawked at the governess.

"Close your mouth, dear, and answer the question," Miss Tibbles said, almost kindly.

Penelope knew the governess too well to be deceived. "Perhaps I should leave," she said nervously.

"Oh, no," Miss Tibbles retorted. "Since you are generally privy to your sister's thoughts, I should like you to stay and hear what I have to say as well."

As one, the twins sank onto the edge of the bed and waited nervously.

"I am waiting," Miss Tibbles reminded her charge.

"It is a trick, I am certain," Rebecca said warily.

"And if it is? Does that change anything?" Miss Tibbles asked mildly. "After all, I have offered to help. You must tell me how."

She waited and when Rebecca still did not answer she went on, her voice rising, "Perhaps we should begin with the question of what you were doing in the street, in the first place. There were, I noticed, several such details you left out of the account you gave your parents. You will not get away with such nonsense with me."

Rebecca shivered and Miss Tibbles nodded to herself with satisfaction. She waited, and with a sigh, Rebecca tried to explain.

"I wished to go out by myself. And I took my abigail with me, Miss Tibbles. I know it is not generally done, but I thought there would be no real harm in it. I did not go very far."

"Why not wait for me to accompany you?"

Rebecca hesitated. It was a question to which she had no answer. How could she explain her restlessness to Miss Tibbles when she did not understand it herself?

Miss Tibbles attempted to fill the gap of silence. "You feel somehow that there is something lacking in your life, perhaps? That there is not enough to do? Perhaps you were even looking for some sort of romantic encounter?"

"Rebecca!" Penelope said in shocked tones. "Surely not? We did agree, didn't we, that we would never marry? That we would never fall prey to romantical emotions the way our sisters did."

Rebecca ignored the sarcastic quality of her governess's voice and the indignation in Penelope's. Instead, she swallowed hard and looked at Miss Tibbles as she said, her voice scarcely above a whisper, "Yes. All those things. It is so lonely without Diana and Annabelle and Barbara."

Penelope gasped again with indignation, but the expression on Miss Tibbles's face softened and she came to sit beside Rebecca. She even put an arm around the girl's shoulders. "I know," she said softly. "You still have your twin, Penelope, but your other sisters are all gone and you don't know what you will do with your own life. You are torn between girlhood and womanhood, and everything is uncertain."

Rebecca turned to her gratefully. "You do understand, then!"

Miss Tibbles nodded. Her voice, however, became stern as she rose to her feet and said, "Yes, I do, but that does not excuse your behavior. As penance you will write me an essay upon the reasons it is imperative for a girl to follow the dictates of propriety, regardless of how she feels. And if it is not, in my opinion, satisfactory, you will do it again until it is. Is that clear?"

"Yes, Miss Tibbles."

"Good."

The governess started to leave the room and Rebecca stopped her. "Miss Tibbles?"

"Yes?"

"I truly am happy the stranger is going to stay."

Miss Tibbles hesitated. "I know," she said.

The look in Rebecca's eyes was enough, however, to make her turn away to hide the brief glimmer of moisture in her own eyes. Governesses, after all, do not cry.

She tried to tell herself that it was admirable that Rebecca wished to help someone less fortunate than herself. Miss Tibbles certainly did not wish to inhibit charitable impulses. But it would have been so much easier if Rebecca had chosen a woman to aid.

On the other hand, Miss Tibbles also told herself consolingly, what real harm could there be? To be sure, the *ton* might look askance at such impulsiveness, but it was not fatal. Not for the daughter of an earl. For the daughter of an earl, whose father possessed a fortune, it would be seen as a charming eccentricity.

Such was Miss Tibbles's cynicism about the world. No, she was troubled more by the mere fact that this fellow was a man and Rebecca seemed quite drawn to him. Still, he was a ruffian, a street creature, totally without the redeeming qualities of breeding, a fortune, or even a handsome face. Rebecca was a sensible girl. Surely she could not truly feel a *tendre* for the fellow? Especially since she would see him at close quarters and must soon realize how ordinary he was.

Rarely had Miss Tibbles been so wrong.

Chapter 3

In the short time she had been in London, Rebecca had already collected one bird with a broken wing, an injured cat, and a squirrel that would eat out of her hand. And now a vagabond.

Rebecca saw him before he saw her. He was in the garden working when she went out to check on the bird and cat and squirrel.

He looked so gaunt, as though he had not eaten well of late, that she wished she had thought to bring out food to him. But all she had in her basket was food for her animals. Besides, she tried to tell herself, now that he was working here at the house, he would be well fed. Still, it didn't stop Rebecca from wishing she could give him the food with her own hands.

His clothes were much improved as well. No doubt Papa or Aunt Ariana had insisted he bathe. And change into the household colors. Someone had even made an attempt to trim his fair hair. And yet he still somehow looked like a wild creature, one who could never be entirely tamed.

Rebecca tried to be quiet. But even as she stood there watching him, he turned, saw her, and smiled before he could stop himself. Because he wanted to stop himself. That much was clear from the way he looked swiftly away, then tried to scowl at her. Only the scowl didn't take. An upward quiver of his mouth insisted on denying it. As did his eyes. Indeed, they looked at her with so much warmth she seemed to glow from it.

He was so tall, Rebecca thought. He could not help but tower over her. And she had no doubt he could have broken her in two without the least effort. His hands alone were far larger than her own.

But for all his attempts to look so fierce, Rebecca didn't believe he would ever hurt anyone on purpose. Unless they deserved it, of course. Still, his fists were tightly clenched at his sides and perhaps it would be prudent to stay out of reach of them.

Rebecca waited for him to speak first. He didn't. She swallowed and said, softly, "I'm so glad Aunt Ariana gave you a position here. I told you she would."

When he still didn't speak, she went on, "I know it must all be very new to you, and not entirely comfortable. But it will be, soon. And then you will be very glad you have come here."

Something shifted in his expression. His eyes seemed almost hooded as he replied, in a voice she wasn't certain she was supposed to hear, "Will oi? Oi wonder."

Rebecca forgot her fear and stepped forward. She set down her basket of food for the animals and took one of his hands in hers, easing it open. It dwarfed her own.

"You will," she assured him. "I shall do everything I can to help you adjust, to succeed in the post you have undertaken."

Now it seemed she had amused him. He did not trouble to hide his grin. Or try to draw his hand away from hers. "Will you?" he asked. " 'Ow, m'lydie? 'Ow can yer 'elps the loikes o' me?"

But she wouldn't let him shake her. "I don't know," she said, "but I swear that I will."

He did pull his hand free now, and his voice was hoarse as he took a step away. "Oi don'ts wants no 'elp. Oi don'ts need no 'elp."

He meant to hurt her with his words. To push her away.

To set a distance between them. Rebecca was certain of it. But she wouldn't let him do it.

Wisely, softly, with utter kindness, Rebecca said, "Yes, you do."

He looked at her then, and there was a mixture of exasperation and rueful humor in the depths of his deep blue eyes as he looked into hers. "You can'ts 'elp me," he repeated.

Rebecca just shook her head. She smiled. "Of course I can!" she said mischievously. "You just don't know it yet. But I'll prove it to you. I swear I will."

That seemed to alarm him. He took a step backward. Rebecca followed. He took another step backward. And then a third. And then he fell over a barrel placed too close to the path.

Instantly, Rebecca was on her knees beside him, stroking the side of his cheek. The man groaned and closed his eyes. Dear Lord! Was he hurt worse than she thought?

She asked the question aloud.

Hurt? The girl wanted to know if he was hurt? Rowland groaned again and opened his eyes. "Oi'm foine," he said disgustedly. "Oi just needs to gets to me feet."

She didn't even have the sense to let him manage that himself. She insisted on trying to help him up. With an inward sigh, Rowland scrambled to his feet before she over tipped herself and landed on top of him. While he had no doubt it would be a delicious feeling for him, he also had no doubt it would shock her terribly to find herself pressed so intimately against a man.

Which might not be such a bad thing. What the devil was he going to do if she insisted on dogging his footsteps? He was supposed to be watching the street, not chattering with a girl scarcely out of the schoolroom!

He tried to bring himself to be harsh to her. "Oi've work

to do, m'lydie," he said. "Oi'll thank yer to let me get on to it."

There was a catch in her voice, that tugged at his heart and made him feel the veriest beast as she said, "Very well, I shall let you alone. For now. But remember. No matter what happens, you have a friend in this house. And I do mean to help you, any way I can, whether you believe me or not."

He merely grunted in reply, not letting her see that he was oddly touched by her words. It had been a long time since anyone wanted to take care of Hugh Rowland, rather than the other way around, and it was a very curious sensation. One he could far too easily grow accustomed to liking.

But how could she take care of him, he asked himself. She couldn't even take care of herself. Look at the danger she had gotten into just this morning.

And yet he was touched that she cared. That she wanted to try. But he didn't want to be touched. He didn't want to care what she thought or felt. He wanted to remain as harsh and aloof as he had learned so long ago to be.

She must have seen something in his face that frightened her because abruptly Lady Rebecca snatched up her basket and continued toward the back of the garden. Unable to stop himself, he followed.

There he saw her kneel down to hand-feed a small bird she had in a cage and then a cat, cradled in a basket nearby. They were makeshift homes for the creatures, and he guessed her family did not want the animals inside. Finally, he watched in amazement as she coaxed a squirrel to come and take some food from her hand.

"Wotcher doin'?" he asked when she finally got to her feet again.

She looked at him, a mixture of concern and defiance in her face as she said, "I've no doubt it seems very foolish to you, but someone must take care of poor, helpless creatures like these."

As he had once done. And been laughed at for it by his parents and his brother. Odd how much Lady Rebecca looked like his first love, Felicity, and yet how different she was in character. Odd how easily she seemed to be able to make a place for herself in his thoughts and, perhaps even, his heart.

But he daren't think about that. Instead, Hugh looked at the tattered basket with the cat and something troubled him. He knelt down. After a moment he looked at Lady Rebecca and said, "She's 'bout to 'ave kittens, she is."

"What? How can you tell?"

Rowland grinned at the astonishment in her voice. So there was something Lady Rebecca didn't know. He showed her how to feel the cat's side, gently, so that she could also feel the kittens moving around inside.

"When?" she asked.

"Soon."

"Oh, I wish I had a better place for her," Lady Rebecca said, rising to her feet again. "Something to hold the kittens as well! She won't be able to keep them with her in the basket, nor follow them about. Not with her leg injured as it is."

Hugh frowned, thinking. She misunderstood. Unshed tears sparkled in her eyes as she said defiantly, "I can see you think me absurd for caring. Every one else does. But I don't care! I will take care of them. But for now, I shan't disturb you any further. Good day!"

He watched as she stalked off back to the house. Already his mind was working, calculating when he would have time to build her a box for the cat.

That he cared as much about Lady Rebecca as he did about the animals she wanted to help, was something Hugh wasn't ready to admit even to himself.

Later, much later, well after dark, Rowland slipped out of the house. He was already late for his appointment with

Sir Parker, but there was no help for it. The major domo, Jeffries, had turned out to be a remarkably light sleeper.

He paused at the front of the house, then plunged forward toward the now deserted street. To be sure, there were torches lit by some of the front doors, but if he were quick about it, no one was likely to see him. Or so he thought.

Hugh had not gone three houses when several figures stepped out of the shadows by a house Rowland had already noticed was untenanted. One of the figures, a fellow who was taller and outweighed him by a fair margin, grabbed him by the collar and hauled him up on his toes.

Behind him, a harsh voice asked, "Wot are you doing out 'ere at noight? And wot are you doing in that 'ouse'old, sudden loike, when you was on the street just this morning?"

"Wot's yer game?" another voice put in.

Rowland almost grinned. He sensed, however, that at the moment it would not be the wisest of moves. Instead, he said, in his cockiest voice, "Oi've gots me a job. In a swell's 'ouse'old. Wot's it ter you?"

"Why? 'Ow?" the first voice demanded.

Rowland tried to shrug. "Oi saved a young lydie of the 'ouse. Didn't mean to. Just instinct, oi guess. Anyways, them swells was roight eager to give me a post. Oi took it. For as long as it pleases me."

"That's all to it?"

Now Rowland let his expression turn sly. "All oi'll say," he agreed. "Oi moights 'ave sumfing more in mind."

"Thieving, you means?"

Rowland winked. "Oi won'ts say no an' oi won'ts say yes. Oi will say as 'ow oi keeps me peepers open."

"'Ere now! 'E can't steal from that 'ouse. 'E does and e's poaching on our territory!" someone else protested.

Rowland listened to the growing grumbling around him with delight. It was going perfectly. Taking a post in Lady Brisbane's household might have been the best thing he could have done, judging by what was being said around him.

The next voice, however, wiped away his cockiness. It was far too serious.

"Kill 'im."

"Woi?" Rowland let himself squeak.

"Loike 'e said, you're poaching on our territory," the first voice said.

Rowland pretended to think. "Can'ts you use an extra bloke?" he asked, trying to sound anxious.

Someone took a step toward Rowland. Another held up a hand to forestall a confrontation. A third asked the question on all their minds, "Woi'd you want to join up wif us?"

Rowland shrugged. "Oi don'ts," he said. "But oi don'ts want to run foul 'un you, neither."

That made sense to the men. They wouldn't want to run foul of themselves either. The first fellow rubbed his chin thoughtfully. He signaled to the giant holding Rowland to let him go. "We'll thinks about it," he said. "And lets you know. Meanwhile, don'ts even think about crossing us."

Rowland pretended to try to smile, then let it trail off as if it was something he couldn't quite manage. He pretended to try to swagger, not very successfully.

They didn't stop him when he began to walk away, and Hugh let himself get to the corner before he let them see him begin to run. The sound of their laughter followed him up the street.

He could scarcely believe his good fortune. It had gone exactly as he wanted. And now to get to his rendezvous with Sir Parker.

Rowland moved through the darkness swiftly, avoiding street lights and the attention of anyone he passed. It was half an hour later when, having finally lost the man who had been trailing him, he knocked at the rear door of a neat Georgian-style house in Mayfair.

A servant, who did not seem in the least surprised or disconcerted to see him, despite his strange appearance, let Rowland in and led him upstairs to the elegantly appointed study that had clearly never seen a lady's hand. The colors were dark and the chairs deep and comfortable.

Hugh had only moments to wait before Sir Parker himself appeared. He took one look at Rowland's face and went straight over to where a tray with brandy stood waiting.

Sir Parker poured him a drink. He then poured one for himself and, when they were both seated, abruptly said, "Well?"

Rowland grinned. He related his day's adventures, leaving out nothing except his own curious empathy with Lady Rebecca. He told himself it didn't matter, that he had never let his emotions interfere with his work before and that he certainly wouldn't begin now. Instead, he focused on the group he had encountered just before he came here.

"And you think the men who accosted you are the men we seek?" Sir Parker asked.

Hugh nodded. "It seems most likely. One was the fellow who was being chased this morning. Another I'm certain I saw hanging about to meet him. They seemed reluctant to come to a decision about me on their own, as if they need to consult with someone. So, yes, I think this could be our quarry—if your information is right that this square was to be their next target."

Sir Parker's expression turned grim. "It is," he said. "We heard it from two different sources. Very well. So you've a post in that house. What good will it do if they're already done with that square?"

Rowland shook his head. "I don't think they are. Otherwise, why would they still have been hanging around? Besides, the servants in Lady Brisbane's household said the thief hadn't succeeded in getting whatever it was he came for. He had to drop it to escape. No, I think they'll be back.

And if what you've told me is correct, they often target more than one house at a time anyway."

He paused and his smile took a very nasty turn as he added, "If we're very lucky, they may even decide to target Lady Brisbane's house. And I shall be in a position to help them."

Sir Parker shook his head but he did not disagree. On the contrary, he agreed only too well. Abruptly he asked, "What do you think of the Westcotts? Any chance one of them is involved?"

Hugh pondered the question, then shook his head. "No. There's only the earl himself, all the rest of the family is female. And he, by all accounts, is far too honorable to take part in such a thing as this. And too old. From what you've told me, I should guess this to be a young man's game."

"There are sons-in-law," Sir Parker objected.

Again Rowland shook his head. "I've heard all about them. The eldest daughter married the Duke of Berenford, of whom the wildest thing I've heard is that he once masqueraded as a common groom. The second married Lord Winsborough and he was killed by highwaymen. Then she married Lord Winsborough."

"Excuse me?"

Hugh waved a hand. "Never mind, neither Winsborough was the sort to indulge in such a thing as this. Now, the third daughter married Viscount Farrington, and he has, at times, been considered quite notorious. But I know Farrington from the war. I give you my word that he could not be caught up in this either. As for the two youngest daughters, they are still at home."

And God help him if Sir Parker asked his opinions of them! What could he say? That one hated men and the other was the dearest creature he had ever seen? But Sir Parker didn't ask. He was still thinking of the men in the family.

"That tallies with my own notions," Sir Parker agreed. "I

know Lord Westcott, just a little, and he has always seemed to me to be an honorable man."

"Then why the devil did you ask me all this?"

"Because I might have been wrong," Sir Parker said mildly. "I always like to check my impressions against those of people I trust."

It was a compliment, and Hugh took it as such. He grinned. "The only drawback of my new situation," he said, "is that I look more reputable than I would like."

Sir Parker snorted. "You needn't fear. You still don't look in the least like a gentleman!"

Rowland laughed. He tossed off the rest of his brandy and rose to his feet. "I'd best be on my way. If anyone in that household realizes I'm gone, I'll really be in the suds."

"In a moment. What do you say to giving these men you met tonight something more to help them believe you are indeed a thief?" Sir Parker asked thoughtfully.

"Such as?" Hugh countered, his eyes twinkling.

"Suppose you were to slip out of the house, and by what you've told me, it is possible, and manage to pick the pockets of one of my men?"

Rowland nodded slowly. "It's an excellent notion. When and where?"

They settled the details between them. Of necessity there had to be a wide allowance for time. Still, they thought it could be done. Sir Parker walked Hugh to the back door, joking all the way about how much more useful Rowland would be to him, now that he was acquiring the skills of a servant as well as a thief and spy.

Then, suddenly serious, Sir Parker said, "Be careful, my boy."

Equally serious, Hugh replied, "I always am."

He meant it. He had survived too many years by doing just that. He would take care against the ring of thieves, and he would take care against Lady Rebecca. For though he would never have said so to Sir Parker, she, he thought, was the greater danger to him now.

She tempted him to begin to trust. She tempted him to begin to believe in gentleness and kindness and goodness again. And if he did, he might forget how to be cynical and dangerous himself. And that would never do.

Chapter 4

Rebecca sat at the window of the bedroom she shared with Penelope. She could not sleep. Somewhere in the house *he* was asleep. She hadn't even thought to ask his name and, as far as she could tell, neither had anyone else. Except perhaps the servants, and she could scarcely ask them without occasioning even more comment than she already had.

But now, at this late hour, Rebecca wondered. Who was he? Where had he grown up? How had he come to be on the square these past few days? And how long would he be willing to stay beneath this roof?

How she wished she knew more about him! To be sure, he had, by all accounts, done as he was bid today. But Rebecca did not think he was a biddable man. She couldn't help wondering what he really thought. Or how he really felt.

She also couldn't help thinking of how soft his face had felt beneath her fingertips. Or the way his hand had felt in hers. Indeed, she trembled as she recalled how close they had stood to one another, outside the back door.

And as much as she wondered about the stranger, Rebecca wondered even more about herself and the emotions he roused in her. For they went far beyond the desire to help him that she had confessed to Miss Tibbles.

What was wrong with her, that she could feel these things about a man who was a stranger? A man who was

not even of her own social class. Why did she ache to touch
his arm, his hand, his face again? Why did she long, so
foolishly, for him to touch her? It was madness!

If Mama ever knew, ever guessed—but she would not.
Rebecca would see to that. And yet, when she pressed her
hands to her cheeks she could feel they were flushed and
warm.

A sound came from the bed where Penelope was sleeping. Rebecca turned and looked at her sister and flushed
again. Beyond everything else, what she was thinking, what
she was feeling, was a betrayal of her twin. For hadn't she
sworn that she would never allow any man to turn her
head?

Granted, she and Penelope had been speaking of men of
their social class, but it was a betrayal all the same. Hadn't
she promised that she would never allow any fellow to oc-
cupy her thoughts for more than two moments at a time?
And this stranger was. Oh, how he was occupying her
mind.

Rebecca rested her head on her knees, drawn up close to
her chest. She held tightly to them and knew that she
longed to clasp something, no, someone else.

There was no one, of course, she could talk to about how
she felt. Her mother and father and aunt would be appalled.
Penelope would never understand. Miss Tibbles would forbid her to ever see the stranger again and would see that he
was dismissed from the house. And her older sisters were
gone.

Down below, in the tiny garden, something caught Rebecca's eye. Was someone there? Hope, a tiny spark of it,
began to glow inside her. She saw it again. Someone was
definitely down in the garden.

It did not occur to Rebecca that there could be danger.
Somehow she knew it was he, and she had to see him.
Maybe it was the way he tilted his head as he looked up to-
ward the house. Maybe it was the way he scuffed at the dirt

with his foot. What respectable thief, planning to break into the house, would do that?

Her robe already tied tightly around her, Rebecca fairly flew down the servants' stairwell that led to the back door. Her footsteps were almost silent, for she was barefoot. She unlocked the door and stepped outside, careful not to make a sound as she did so.

There he was! He hadn't seen her yet. He was gazing at the upper stories of the house, as though looking for her window, she told herself. She tiptoed toward him, without a sound, she was certain. But still he heard her.

He turned, swiftly, almost frightening her with the way he moved. And before Rebecca could decide whether to advance or retreat, he was upon her.

He pulled her up sharply against him and his hand clamped over her mouth in a way that was rough. "Are you mad!" he hissed. "Coming out here at night like this?"

She didn't notice the way he spoke. She should have, but she didn't. Instead, she held very still. And waited. When she didn't move, didn't try to answer, didn't try to escape, he slowly lifted his hand from her mouth.

When she still didn't speak, he gave a sigh of exasperation. And held her close against him as she rested her head against his chest.

She could feel him breathing. Harshly. As though his breath came in gasps. She looked up at him with luminous eyes and he stared down at her like a man haunted by some ghost he wished were real but didn't dare credit.

At least that was the way it seemed to Rebecca. She reached up and plucked at his sleeve with her hand.

"Please don't be angry with me," she said. "I noticed you out here and I had to come down. I thought, I hoped, you would be happy to see me."

With a groan, he bent forward and rested his forehead against hers. Rebecca moved her hand from his sleeve to stroke the side of his face. He turned and kissed her palm.

She shivered then, in the cool night air, and he noticed. He tried to step away from her. But he didn't go very far, and Rebecca felt a hint of triumph.

"Something is troubling you," she said softly. "What is it? What are you afraid of?" she asked softly.

"You."

It was the truth. Whatever else she doubted about the man, Rebecca did not doubt that. And yet it was not all of the truth. Something else troubled him. Something beyond being here with her. She had sensed it from the moment she had seen him on the street, waiting for someone to pay him a penny to sweep the cobblestones. Someday she would make him tell her what it was. But for now she would play the game he chose, and pretend there was nothing more to it than what he said.

"I am not afraid of you," she countered boldly.

He took a long, shuddering breath. "You should be," he said fiercely.

"You would never hurt me," she said with the assurance of a woman twice her age.

But her words seemed to make him angry, as though she had opened an old wound. As though he wanted to believe them but he couldn't. He pushed her away. He meant to do it roughly, she sensed that much. Instead, his touch was gentle and lingered a moment longer than he wanted.

"Wot are you afraid of, m'lydie?" he asked, his voice almost tender. "Anyfing?"

But perhaps the tenderness was only in her imagination. Everyone said she had far too much of it. "I'm afraid of many things," she told him with a smile.

"Loike wot?"

Rebecca let her fingertips touch a nearby bush, one that would be flowering soon. "I'm terribly afraid of disappointing my parents," she said with a wry smile. "Of forgetting some rule when I am out amongst the *ton*. I know that must seem very silly to you, but in my world it matters dearly."

"It don't sound silly," he said gruffly. "Wot else?"

She let go of the bush and twisted the skirt of her dressing gown with her fingers. It was so hard to put into words what she feared. And yet, this was someone whom it was safe to tell, precisely because he was not of her world.

"I'm afraid of getting married. Of finding myself tied to someone who doesn't care about me and whom I discover, too late, that I dislike. Sometimes I think it would be far easier to spend my days here, with my sister and family, and the animals I've rescued, than to ever marry. And I think I have more in common with someone like you than someone of my own class."

That truly did startle him, and abruptly he turned, as though frightened by her words. "'Oi've gots to be going now," he said, and hurried toward the house. "Oi'll lose me place if they catches me out 'ere wif yer. No, nor you oughtn't to be out 'ere, neither."

"Wait!" she said softly. He hesitated just a moment, long enough for her to ask, "What is your name?"

To her surprise, and perhaps his own, he answered, "Hugh."

Then, with a muttered curse, he came back and grabbed her hand and pulled her inside the house with him. "Go on up," he told her, giving Rebecca a little shove toward the back stairway. "It ain't safe out 'ere, late loike it is. Oi'll be roight up, meself, but oi ain'ts gettin' caught wif the loikes of you, m'lydie."

She went. And halfway up remembered and wondered about the difference between the soft, almost educated way he had spoken when she first appeared and the rough way later. Was he trying to imitate what he had heard in this house? Oh, how she hoped it was so!

Slowly, quietly, Rebecca made her way to her room, hugging that hope and his name to herself. Softly she whispered it out loud. "Hugh."

It was a name that suited him. She whispered it again as

she climbed into bed and pulled the covers over herself. She whispered it a third time just before she fell asleep.

Unfortunately, neither Rebecca nor Hugh remembered to lock the door behind them.

It was hours later. Close to dawn. Upstairs, couples still whirled in a riotous dance at this less than reputable house in London. But in this room, the candlelight flickered. A group of men sat in shadows. One giggled. Another shushed him instantly. All but one of them wore hoods. In the center of the ring was a man Hugh Rowland would have recognized easily. He was the one not wearing a hood, and his expression was clearly pugnacious.

"Oi thoughts we ought to speak to 'im. Oi thoughts you ought to know wot 'e was about," he said, daring anyone to challenge him. Only one man did.

"How enterprising of you. To risk our possible anger this way. Still, perhaps you were right to do so. You have given us a most interesting report. It almost outweighs your failure on that other little matter."

The man in the middle of the room shivered. "Oi tolds you. We troied. 'Tweren't our fault they was loighter sleepers than we thought. Tiny troied to 'oide 'til morning, but there weren't no way for 'im to get out unseen. Give us another chance, guv'nor. I promise we'll get it roight next toime!"

For a long moment there was no answer. It was a silence most of the men in the room, and certainly the man in the middle, were reluctant to break. Then the voice came again. Abrupt. Certain.

"No. You won't do a thing until I tell you. Except to bring this man to me. I want to see him. Two nights from now. At midnight. You know the place."

The man in the middle of the circle nodded. He knew, all right. And he smiled an evil smile, for there was something about the man they had questioned tonight that he just did not like. He ignored the voices that rose all around the room. Their disagreements, after all, were none of his affair. They gave him information and he used it to steal what they told him to steal. Anything else was between them.

"I can't make it that night!" someone protested.

"I thought we weren't supposed to meet again for a couple of weeks!" another said. "Besides, we want the money those jewels would have brought, not another fellow to share the prize."

And so it went. Finally the voice spoke again, the one that gave the orders. Softly, dangerously, it asked, "Have I said that anyone other than myself need attend?"

Silence.

"I didn't think so. I will go alone. I will make the decision alone. You, all of you, need not disturb your pleasures for this."

The contempt in the voice lashed out at them, and everyone, save the one who spoke and the man in the center, flinched. One voice, however, dared to challenge the first.

"What is all the fuss about this fellow. There are vagabonds all over London trying to beg or earn their way. Why bother with even one of them?"

In the shadows the leader noted the one who had spoken. They were all supposed to be anonymous to one another, but of course they weren't anonymous to him. He had recruited each and every one of them, and a skill at knowing voices had stood him in good stead since he began this venture. Now he mentally chalked out the name Philip Caldwell, for that was who had challenged him.

Softer than before, so that each man present had to strain to hear and understand him, the leader spoke. "Why do I bother? Because this man could be useful to us. And I do not turn away useful tools. He could also be a danger. You have heard our friend say he had the feeling there was something odd about the man. And his interest in joining them."

"A feeling!" the same rebel spoke, contempt fairly dripping from the word.

Undeterred, the leader smiled beneath his hood and the smile showed in his voice as he said, "I have long since learned to trust the instincts of a man like this one. I will see this vagabond and would-be thief. Rest assured, he will either become one of us or I will make certain he is not a threat."

The leader did not say how he would make certain. It would not do, after all, to frighten away the newest members of his group. One or two would come to accept death as easily as he did, but most were not ready yet, and never would be. Still, he was pleased to see that no one, not even Philip Caldwell, demanded to know what he meant to do. Good. That meant they were learning.

When he was satisfied the silence had gone on long enough, the leader said to the man standing in the center of the room, "You may go."

And when the thief had exited by the secret door, the leader stood. Beneath his hood he smiled again as he said softly, "Now the rest of you will go, one by one, out of this room, in the prescribed order, at the prescribed intervals of time. You will leave your hoods and cloaks, as always, in the outer room here and join the party taking place above our heads. And we will meet again as planned. You will receive precise instructions as to the place and time in the usual way."

Chapter 5

The house was in an uproar.

"Is anything missing?" Lady Westcott asked her sister anxiously.

"Not that I can discover," Lady Brisbane replied tremulously.

"Don't worry, we'll check everything out," Lord Westcott assured them both stoutly.

Penelope watched everything with excitement in her eyes. Rebecca watched everything with a sinking sensation in the pit of her stomach. Miss Tibbles merely watched.

When the bottom-to-top search of the house had ended and everyone was reassured that nothing was missing, the round of pointing blame began.

"Are you absolutely certain you locked all the doors last night?" Lady Brisbane asked her major domo, Jeffries.

"Positive, m'lady," that shaken individual replied.

"What about one of the footmen or one of the serving girls sneaking out to see someone?" Lady Westcott suggested brightly.

"Not in my household!" Lady Brisbane and Jeffries answered together.

Round and round it went. It was inevitable that someone would get around to suggesting the stranger. Hugh hadn't done anything wrong, Rebecca thought with a shudder, but he would be blamed, just the same.

Just as she thought she couldn't bear it any longer and

she was going to have to confess that it was she who had forgotten to lock the door, though how she was to do that without naming Hugh she didn't know, Miss Tibbles stepped forward.

"Perhaps," she said gently, "it was I, when I went downstairs and outside briefly for some fresh air."

Suddenly all conversation stopped in the room. Everyone, including Rebecca, gaped at Miss Tibbles, mouths hanging open. "You?" Lady Westcott asked in disbelief.

"Going out for air in the middle of the night?" Lord Westcott chimed in.

"Why didn't you speak up sooner?" Lady Brisbane demanded.

Miss Tibbles shrugged. "I had forgotten I had done so," she said simply.

One and all they continued to gape. Miss Tibbles? The paragon of common sense and virtue? The woman who was such a bedrock of propriety and stern discipline? The woman who had, in a few short years, already guided three daughters to marriage? And in whose capable hands rested the hope of safely marrying off two more? Impossible!

Finally, Lord Westcott managed to collect himself sufficiently to harrumph, clear his throat, then say, judiciously, "I don't pretend to understand, and I must say that I am most disappointed in you, Miss Tibbles. But I suppose we ought to be happy merely to have the matter settled so easily."

Miss Tibbles nodded and said briskly, "It shan't happen again. And now that we are done with that, I shall take the girls upstairs. There is still time for them to do their lessons this morning."

With bewildered looks at one another, Rebecca and Penelope followed Miss Tibbles out of the room. Penelope kept trying to imagine her governess going downstairs and outside in her night rail. Rebecca tried to imagine why Miss Tibbles had lied. And whether it had been done to protect her. But she wasn't about to ask any questions in front of her sister or, worse, her parents.

Nor did either girl argue with the lessons Miss Tibbles distractedly set before them. Instead, Rebecca waited patiently until the lessons were done and Penelope had her nose safely ensconced in a book. Then Rebecca looked at Miss Tibbles and said, "Could we, perhaps, take a turn in the park do you think?"

"Of course," the governess agreed. "Penelope, I know your dislike for such pointless exercise and your preference for reading, and just this once I think I shall allow you to remain behind."

That alone should have made Penelope suspicious. It should have been more than enough to make her demand to join the others. But the book she was in the midst of reading really was deliciously intriguing and Penelope simply could not put it down, so she nodded and muttered and kept her nose safely where it was. Miss Tibbles and Rebecca hastily fetched their wraps before Penelope could change her mind.

On their way to the park, Rebecca tried to decide how to ask Miss Tibbles the question most strongly on her mind. As it happened, however, there was no need for her to ask anything. It was the governess who broached the matter.

"How dare you behave in such a reckless, feckless way?" Miss Tibbles demanded, walking briskly down the street. "And don't deny it, for your abigail told me she found traces of dirt on the hem of your dressing gown this morning and on your bedsheets."

"If that is what you think, then why did you lie to protect me?" Rebecca demanded.

Miss Tibbles stopped right where she was and looked at Rebecca. There was a softness and a concern in her eyes that the girl had never seen before.

"Oh, my dear Rebecca," Miss Tibbles said, "you remind me so much of me! I hadn't the heart to expose you to your parents' anger. It was quite wrong for me to lie in such a way and I suppose they will have to know the truth, but perhaps after they have calmed down. But I must know, what were you doing outside last night?"

Miss Tibbles started walking again even before she finished speaking, conscious as she was of certain curious eyes upon them. Rebecca hurried to keep up with her governess.

"I don't know," Rebecca answered honestly. "I saw Hugh, the streetsweep Aunt Ariana hired yesterday, from the window and went down to find out why he was there. Only," she paused and frowned, "I never really did. Find out, I mean."

Again, Miss Tibbles halted in her tracks. It took supreme will power for her to start walking again, and the agitation in her voice was unmistakable.

"Do you mean to say that new man was outside as well?" Miss Tibbles asked, appalled. "Had I known that I should never have tried to shield him!" Then a new and even worse thought occurred to her. "If you didn't ask him what he was doing out there, what did the pair of you do?"

"He covered my mouth with his hand, for fear I might scream," Rebecca replied.

"Nothing else?"

"And I touched the side of his face."

With a sinking tone in her voice and her face so pale as to cause Rebecca to feel quite guilty, Miss Tibbles demanded, "Was there anything else?"

"He kissed the palm of my hand."

Now Miss Tibbles's coloring was alarmingly high and it looked to Rebecca as though she might faint at any moment. They had reached the gates of the park and she directed her governess to the nearest empty bench.

"Pray do not alarm yourself," Rebecca said. "Nothing more happened."

"Nothing more?" Miss Tibbles retorted indignantly. "I

consider all of that to have been quite more than enough! My dear Rebecca, when I lied to protect you, I did not think . . . that is to say I assumed . . . Really, had I thought . . . Oh, dear, what on earth am I to do now?"

Helplessly, Rebecca began to pat her governess's hand. "Please, Miss Tibbles, do not be distressed. Truly, there is no need."

"You are not to speak to that man again, Rebecca, do you hear me?" Miss Tibbles said, her voice a trifle shrill. "Otherwise, I shall have to ask your father to dismiss him from Lady Brisbane's staff."

"But that would be most unfair," Rebecca countered softly. "You know I cannot turn my back on someone who needs me as he does."

Miss Tibbles blinked. She puffed up even more in her anger. "Well, why ever not?" she demanded, with pardonable asperity.

"Because you have taught me not to," Rebecca said.

"I?" Miss Tibbles gasped, very much taken aback. "Whatever do you mean?"

Rebecca looked at her governess and said, primly, "You have never turned your back on any of my sisters, even when you would have had good and sufficient reason to do so."

For once, Miss Tibbles was speechless. Bravely, Rebecca went on, "That is one of the reasons we have all come to love you, you know. And I know you will not fail me now."

And then Rebecca hugged Miss Tibbles and had to be told, emphatically, more than once to let her go.

Still, there was a suspicious moisture in that lady's eyes as she said, "Do not think to turn me up sweet this way. It shan't, you know. I shall be watching you most carefully, to make certain such a thing does not happen again."

"Yes, Miss Tibbles."

The governess regarded her sharply, but Rebecca betrayed nothing. Her expression was meek and Miss Tibbles could only hope she meant what she said. Unfortunately, based upon experience, it seemed most unlikely.

Miss Tibbles was not one to leave matters to chance. Not when it was possible for her to take a hand to prevent disaster. It seemed that Rebecca was drawn to the man, more so than she had foreseen. Very well, he could not be dismissed without the girl thinking herself very hardly used. But surely there must be a way to keep them apart?

Miss Tibbles set the girls to their work and then went in search first of Jeffries, to tell him what she meant to do and why, and then she went looking for the new man. She found him sweeping the path behind the house.

How the devil was he going to slip away to carry out Sir Parker's plan? Hugh wondered. They were keeping a far closer watch on him than intended. And for all they had agreed he could go to visit his "mum," if need be, they made it all but impossible.

He was not so lost in his thoughts, however, that he did not hear someone come up behind him. He was prepared, therefore, when a brisk voice interrupted his solitude.

"There you are. I have some errands for you to run. Some things to collect from the shops for me."

Rowland could not stop himself. He whirled around and gawked at the diminutive woman standing before him. The governess. She did not seem surprised by his reaction, but went on in the same brisk voice as before.

"I wish you to collect some parcels for me and I shall give you the directions of each shop. And mind you, don't get up to any tricks in any of those shops, or you will be very sorry. Very sorry, indeed!"

Rowland grinned. Here, at least, was one person who thought him sufficiently disreputable. Still, he had to stay in character. He blinked, shook his head, and croaked out, "Oi wouldn'ts dream of it, ma'am."

The governess smiled beatifically. "Very well, be on your way, then. Oh, and here is a penny for you to purchase something for your midday meal, for you will not be able to return in time to have it here."

Hugh could not help himself. He stared at the coin in her hand for several moments before he tentatively, reluctantly, reached out to take it. Whatever he had expected, it was not this small kindness.

But the woman seemed to think nothing of it. She nodded, smiled encouragingly, and said, "Go along with you now. I have already made certain Jeffries knows where you are going and why. You need not fear to lose your position by doing as I say."

Rowland managed to nod, swallow hard, and then without any further prodding he was on his way. As improbable as it seemed, it looked as if he was going to be able to carry out Sir Parker's plan after all.

Out in the street, Hugh's heart pounded and he felt as though he had just had the narrowest of escapes. He stared at the small coin in his hand. Were they all mad in that household? All convinced they must take every stray creature under their wing? Hastily, he thrust the coin in his pocket. He had work to do, pockets to pick, and no time to lose in doing so.

Hugh had no trouble spotting some of the men he had encountered last night. Good. He would have just the witnesses he needed.

Sir Parker's man was in place, talking to someone down the street. All very natural. And yet waiting for him. He had a lot of practice, Rowland did, and he was able to slip his hand into the man's pocket and lift the bait that had been planted there. That should convince the men watching that he was as disreputable as he seemed.

Then he was away and off to carry out his commissions

for the Westcott governess. All in all, it looked to be a very promising day.

Rebecca, staring out the window, felt sick to her stomach. She could not have just seen what she thought she had seen. He could not have been picking that gentleman's pocket! Not Hugh! Not when she had brought him into this house and pledged to help him.

And yet, neither could she entirely believe she had been wrong.

"Come away from the window, Rebecca!" Penelope, her twin, said urgently. "Miss Tibbles will be back at any moment and you still have not done your sums!"

Reluctantly, Rebecca did so. She, too, heard the footsteps coming down the hall toward them. Quickly, she took her seat and reached for her book of sums. When Miss Tibbles entered, both girls were hard at work. And if there was a hard, bright look in Rebecca's eyes, she did not stop to wonder why.

Chapter 6

It was the next afternoon before a much chastened Rebecca looked in on Hugh as he was polishing andirons in the library. He looked tired, she thought. No doubt he had trouble sleeping in this strange, new place.

She was tempted to go into the library to talk with him, but she didn't dare. Miss Tibbles was watching for just such behavior from her and she would not risk Hugh's place by doing so. And what could she say to him? She could scarcely ask if she had really seen him steal from someone's pocket the day before.

Besides, Rebecca told herself, a gentleman was coming to call and she ought to prepare for that. It was the first time anyone had sent flowers for her, and for Penelope. For all her fears, and however much Penelope disliked it, Rebecca could not resist feeling a swirl of excitement.

To be sure, Aunt Ariana did not truly like this Lord Halifax, and Mama had warned her to be a trifle wary of him, but it was all nonsense! She and Penelope were in London to have a Season and having gentlemen calling and sending flowers was part of it, even if they did set Penelope's teeth on edge and Mama and Aunt Ariana's nerves aflutter.

Rowland noticed the shadow in the doorway of the library and he felt both hope and dismay at the thought that she might come in. For he had no doubt it was Lady Rebecca. A moment later the shadow went away.

So she had decided not to speak with him. It was all for
the best. Of course it was, Hugh told himself firmly as he
polished the andirons for all he was worth. Once this current job was finished, he would have all the time in the
world to speak with her. As it was, if she knew what he was
about, she would probably faint from the shock of it.

That gave him pause, and he stopped polishing. A faint
smile crossed his face. No, she wouldn't faint. She would
probably demand to take part, firmly convinced she was
acting to help someone.

Abruptly, a voice broke into his reverie. "Here now!
Hurry it up! Company for the ladies is expected at any moment and we're all to be below stairs before they come,"
the major domo said from the doorway of the room.

Hugh hastily gathered his things together. No more than
Jeffries did he want to be caught above stairs by company.
Not that anyone in London was likely to recognize him, but
still, he wasn't taking any chances.

"'Oo's coming to calls?" Hugh asked as he came toward
the major domo.

Jeffries raised his eyebrows in reproof, but he did answer. "A gentleman. Lord Halifax. He sent flowers for
Lady Rebecca and Lady Penelope an hour ago. I expect he
has caught a glimpse of them somewhere and quite liked
what he saw. Now hurry! You'll be wanted in the kitchens
downstairs, I don't wonder."

Hugh went, his expression grim. So Lord Halifax was
coming to call. Did it have anything to do with him? It
needn't, of course. Halifax was a member of the *ton* and
likely to be found calling on other members of the *ton* any
time he wished. Still, it disturbed him.

He would rather, he realized, that Lord Halifax had come
in search of a glimpse of him. Because the thought that he
might have an interest in Lady Rebecca, Hugh discovered,
was intolerable to him. If he did, then Hugh was determined to thrust a spoke in the wheels of whatever plans

Lord Halifax might have for Lady Rebecca. Or Lady Penelope, of course. If their own family didn't know enough to protect them from the rogue, then he would have to do so himself.

As she waited with her mother and aunt and twin in the drawing room, Rebecca felt the most delightful flutter of anticipation. Penelope clearly did not. She sat on a chair, as far away from the others as possible, with a distinct scowl on her face.

"I don't see why Rebecca and I have to do this," she complained bitterly.

"Because it is time for you and Rebecca to look about you for husbands," Lady Westcott said airily. "I have no doubt you will each do as well as your sisters. Indeed, I quite expect it of you."

"I shall never ever marry at all," Penelope pronounced as she rose to her feet, "so there is no reason for me to be here this afternoon. Or Rebecca. She is never going to marry either."

"Never marry? Nonsense, you will both marry. Now sit down again," Lady Westcott commanded.

Penelope stared at her mother mulishly and continued to stand. Lady Brisbane took pity on her niece and said quietly, "Well, Penelope, you are free to leave the room, of course, but don't you think your sister, Rebecca, needs your support? Particularly when Lord Halifax has been so kind as to send flowers to both of you? Surely you would wish to be here to form your own opinion of the fellow? Suppose he should ask to take Rebecca for a drive? Do you not wish to go along to lend her countenance? Of course, if need be, your mother or I could do so."

That was enough. More than enough. As Rebecca watched with a hastily suppressed grin, Penelope sat down again and said, "No, no, if Rebecca needs me, I shall stay.

Just as she would stay for me. Someone must keep an eye on things," she added darkly.

Now Rebecca suppressed a sigh. She loved her twin dearly, but it was very hard that Penelope was so opposed to men.

There was a sound in the hallway. Rebecca didn't need the silent signal from her mother to quickly take a seat and arrange her skirts becomingly. Or to smile at the door while she pretended to converse with Aunt Ariana. Her pulse beat rapidly at her throat. Lord Halifax was her first real caller, a grown man, not a callow youth simply curious to see the latest additions to the London Marriage Mart. Rebecca wondered what he would be like.

On the surface, Lord Halifax was all that was amiable as he entered the room. He bowed first to Aunt Ariana and Mama, as was only proper. And he allowed them to introduce him to Rebecca and Penelope. The way he bowed to Rebecca was perfectly proper and correct and he smiled as though he found her charming.

But the smile, Rebecca thought, did not quite reach his eyes. Indeed, there was something in his eyes that almost frightened her. Or would have, had she not been surrounded by her loving family. And a moment later it was gone anyway, replaced by calm serenity as he sat and chatted with them all, endeavoring even to draw Penelope into the conversation. Perhaps it was his kindness to her twin that led Rebecca to warm her heart, at least a little, to the man.

And when he asked to take both of them for a drive in the park, she was perfectly willing to agree. Especially as Mama and Lady Brisbane smiled at Lord Halifax approvingly.

Penelope regarded his lordship with the expression of a martyr headed for the stake and Rebecca had to fight hard not to laugh at the sight. But even she could not long resist the joy of being out on a bright sunny day riding behind a beautiful pair of matched bays.

Halifax was content. It was probably a waste of time to be doing this, but he had never been one to disdain even the faintest advantage such a step could bring him. He liked to be prepared. The new man he was to see tonight was a member of the Brisbane/Westcott household. One of Lord Westcott's daughters had brought him home. That much his sources had told him. Now he wished to see if he could learn anything more.

It would be convenient if he knew which girl had brought the man home, but it really didn't matter. Either one might tell him something useful.

Halifax had brought his finest horses, hoping to impress the two young ladies. They were smiling and, he hoped, unaware as he said, casually, "I understand, ladies, that one of you has generous heart."

"How so?" Lady Rebecca asked cautiously.

She answered cautiously, but then Halifax had always enjoyed a challenge. Now he shrugged. "Oh, I have heard that one of you rescued some poor fellow from the streets and gave him a place in your home."

Both young ladies stiffened, but that was only to be expected, Halifax told himself. Nor did he mind the coldness in Lady Rebecca's voice as she replied, "On the contrary, he rescued me! I took him home for Papa to properly thank him and Papa decided he would be handy to have about the house. Aunt Ariana agreed."

"Of course." Halifax kept his voice deliberately soothing. "Still, it seems a risky thing to do—to keep a fellow from the streets, one presumably without references, in one's household."

"I assure you, he is watched very closely," she retorted.

Was that a hint of bitterness in her voice? Had she a bit of softness for the fellow? Well, it did not matter to Halifax. Was the man perhaps shrewd enough to exploit whatever opportunity he could? If so, Halifax admired the fellow for being able to do so. No, he had other concerns.

"Where is he from, do you know?" Halifax persisted.

Lady Rebecca started to answer and then abruptly, she closed her mouth. Penelope answered for her. "We don't know anything about the man," she said tartly. "As Papa says, what is there to know about a fellow from the streets? No doubt he was born in some alleyway here in London. That's what Papa says."

But Halifax did not think he had been. For if the man had grown up in London, it was likely their paths would have crossed before now.

Still, there was no point in pressing the issue. Clearly the two young ladies knew very little, after all, about the man. Instead he said lightly, "I don't suppose you would let me hire him away from you?"

"Why?" Penelope demanded. "What would you want with the fellow?"

"You would have to speak with Papa, or Aunt Ariana," Rebecca chimed in sweetly. "It is absurd to think that my sister or I would have any say in such matters."

Halifax could have bitten his tongue. "Of course," he said smoothly. "It is just that, well, I had thought perhaps you were fond of the fellow, Lady Rebecca."

She laughed. He could not tell if the laugh were genuine, but it seemed to be. "How absurd!" she said. "As if I would bother myself about a mere servant."

Well, there was that, Halifax thought. However odd the circumstance of his rescuing her and her taking him home, it did seem most unlikely. Very well, so he had learned nothing new, discovered no new vantage point to hold over the fellow. It was still useful to have a welcome in the Westcott household, a way to discover if something came to light about the man. Halifax did not consider his time wasted in the slightest. But it was time to draw this nonsense to a close. He would take them both home on amiable terms, and maintain some contact with the household.

Aloud he said, "Of course, Lady Rebecca. How foolish of me to think otherwise." A pause then, with some concern, "My dear Lady Penelope, are you all right? You look a trifle pale. Let me take you home at once."

"I am perfectly all right!" she exclaimed indignantly.

"But Penny, if there is the least doubt, we should go home," Rebecca said, with equal concern.

It was adroitly done. Halifax would not sever the connection, because it still might prove of use. Indeed, it would be convenient to be given the run of the house. But he had no interest in really dangling after infants. He made his plans as he turned the carriage around.

After he escorted the girls home he would take a moment to drop a gold coin into the major domo's fist and request that word be sent to him if the man he was interested in was ever turned off.

Rebecca was most anxious about Penelope. Still, once they were home, she seemed to recover swiftly. Mama and Lady Brisbane, after bestowing searching looks upon Rebecca and her sister, turned their attention to Lord Halifax, with a desire to please him. So well did they succeed, or so well had his fancy already been taken by one or both girls, that before he took his leave, Lord Halifax promised to arrange to have invitations sent to Rebecca and Penelope for his sister's ball.

"It is terribly late of me to do so, I know," Halifax said in a self-deprecating way. "Had I known Lady Rebecca and Lady Penelope were so charming, I would certainly have made their acquaintance sooner."

He paused and waved a hand airily. "But there it is. I shall do my very best to remedy the oversight at once and invitations to my sister's ball shall be the start of it." He paused again and looked to Lady Westcott. "It is a masquerade. All that is decorous and proper, I assure you. I hope you will allow your lovely daughters to attend?"

"Of course," Lady Westcott agreed, throwing her accustomed wariness over such events to the wind.

"We shall *all* be delighted to attend," Lady Brisbane added, an edge to her voice that was intended to warn Halifax that Penelope and Rebecca would be well chaperoned during the event.

Something crossed his face again but was gone so swiftly that Rebecca could not decide what it meant. Halifax bowed, smiled, said a few more words, and then took his leave.

The moment he was gone Rebecca turned to her mother. Lady Westcott clasped her hands together and all but crowed as she said, "My dearest Rebecca and Penelope, one or both of you have captivated the man! To be sure, you are the daughters of an earl and may expect to have no trouble finding husbands, but still this is an auspicious start. And invitations to his sister's ball! Of all things, the most delightful."

"I thought you said I ought to be wary of the man," Rebecca said to her mother.

Lady Westcott would not meet her daughter's eyes. "Yes, well, of course you ought to be wary of any gentleman. And to be sure Lord Halifax is rumored to have raised any number of expectations without ever actually coming up to scratch. But his attention to you and your sister cannot help but add to your consequence."

"I still don't like him," Lady Brisbane said thoughtfully, "but it would not do to snub him openly. And if he has decided you amuse him and he will undertake to help make you a success, I see no need to spurn his support. Not that you need help. Still, one would not wish to offend Lord Halifax. That would be most unwise. Simply take care not to lose your hearts to the fellow."

"How fortunate the new ballgowns we ordered have already arrived," Lady Westcott said. "And you will wear your pearls, of course. Oh, I vow it will all be so delightful!"

"I won't go to a ball," Penelope vowed, her eyes narrowing in anger. "These small events you have made me attend were bad enough, but I will not, I simply will not, attend a ball. And you cannot force me to."

But of course they did.

Hugh watched Lord Halifax emerge from the drawingroom. He was careful to keep himself out of sight in a doorway, but he watched as the man paused and spoke to Jeffries.

Why the devil was he here? And what was his interest in the Westcott girls? There was a look on the man's face he did not trust. As Halifax went out the front door, Hugh moved over to where he could watch from the window—as he had watched earlier, when Halifax helped Lady Rebecca and Lady Penelope into his carriage to go for a drive.

Hugh did not even notice what he was doing as he twisted and crumpled the curtain edge in his hand. But someone else noticed.

"So you do not like Lord Halifax either," a voice said from behind him.

Hugh spun around and found himself faced by the governess, Miss Tibbles. The terror of the household, according to the servants below stairs.

And yet she was looking at him with a mixture of amusement, approval, and gentle concern in her eyes. She couldn't possibly be as omniscient as all the other servants claimed her to be.

"Oi don'ts know what you mean," Hugh managed to croak.

She tapped her foot impatiently. "I think you do. What's more, I quite agree with you. Not that I have met Lord Halifax personally, but I have heard things. And I do not like what I have heard. Nor do I like the way he looked at my girls. So tell me now, and no lies, what you know of the man to have given you such a dislike of him."

She paused, then added, "It is to protect Lady Rebecca that I am asking."

"Oi'll 'elps if oi can."

Miss Tibbles smiled. "I thought you might."

" 'E 'as a mistress," Hugh could not keep from blurting out.

Miss Tibbles smiled with satisfaction. "I knew you were the right one to ask to help me," she said, nodding approvingly. "Very good. So he has a mistress. What of it? Many gentlemen do."

That was a facer. He tried to think. He had to persuade at least one member of this household to be wary of Halifax and clearly this governess was his most likely prospect.

" 'E watches 'er. Lydie Rebecca. And Lydie Penelope. Not like a gen'lemun wot loikes a lydie, but loike a cat wot watches a mouse," Hugh added.

Miss Tibbles tapped her chin. "I noticed the same thing. Not," she said, drawing herself up to her full height, "that I am in the habit of spying on members of the family, but it seemed a prudent step to take, given rumors I have heard about the man in the past."

Hugh nodded encouragingly and, after a moment, Miss Tibbles added thoughtfully, "What I cannot decide is what his real interest in the girls might be."

It was the same question Hugh had been asking himself. Did the man make a habit of seducing virgins, perhaps? The thought made his blood boil and yet, for all that he disliked the man, he did not think that was it.

His respect for Miss Tibbles grew as he realized just how closely her thoughts matched his own. "I should like to learn everything I can about the man," she said. "And I should like to know that whenever Lady Rebecca and her sister leave the house without their mother or aunt that someone, you if possible, accompanies them. Someone who can watch out for them. I shall speak to Jeffries and I believe it can be arranged."

"Oi'll do me best," Hugh assured the governess quietly, and there was no doubting that he meant what he said. "Oi'll makes sure she stays safe, oi will."

Miss Tibbles looked up at him and said, "I'm sure you will."

Hugh nodded and she turned to leave the room. In the doorway she paused, turned around, and said, "It is a great pity there is such a difference in your stations. Otherwise you are precisely the sort of man I might have wished for Lady Rebecca to find."

At the look that crossed his face she added hastily and with alarm, "It is, however, absolutely out of the question! When you are attempting to keep Lady Rebecca safe, remember that you must keep her safe from yourself as well as from men like Lord Halifax!"

"Yes, ma'am," Hugh replied meekly.

When Miss Tibbles was gone, Hugh could not help replaying her words in his head. They both amused him and alarmed him. Still, he had never encountered a situation he could not handle and he had no reason to believe he could not handle this one as well.

But then, he didn't really know Lady Rebecca, did he?

Chapter 7

Hugh Rowland moved silently through the night. He was not alone, though few other than himself would have known it. They were closing in on him. In a moment he would be surrounded. Still he acted as though he were aware of nothing. He pretended to study a nearby house and the fence as though he planned to climb over it.

"Casing the place, guv'nor?" a voice asked at his elbow.

Hugh turned slowly and shrugged. "P'rhaps. Oi've 'eard tell the lydie 'as some prime sparklers and ear dabs. Moight be worth a look-see."

"Not t'noight," the other countered. He made a signal and several others stepped out of the shadows. He moved closer to Hugh. "T'noight we've someone we wants you to see. Someone wot wants to see you."

Hugh hesitated, as though considering the matter. As though looking around to see how many of them he was facing. Finally he shrugged. "As you loikes. Oi'm an easy-going chap, oi am."

No one actually touched Hugh as they walked down the street, but he had no doubt that if he made any attempt to go anywhere other than where they were leading, someone, probably more than one, would grab him and make him go along. So for now he thrust his hands into his pockets and whistled as though he had not a care in the world.

"Stops that!" his companion hissed.

Hugh pretended surprise. "Woi?"

"Because we don'ts wants no trouble," the other answered. "No, nor no 'un looking at us wot we don'ts wants looking at us," he added. "So mum, now."

Hugh shrugged again and stopped whistling. He still kept his hands in his pockets, however, and pretended complete unconcern though his eyes darted everywhere, noting every turn they took, every alleyway they passed through.

Finally his companion stopped outside a door in one of these alleyways. He signaled with his head to the others, and they all melted away again into the night. Only he and Hugh remained.

A knock. Hugh memorized the pattern, in case it should come in handy later, and waited. Moments later the door opened and the two of them stepped through. Into a deeper darkness than the one outside.

The other took his arm and moved through the darkness as though he could see. Or as though he had been here many times before. Then they were in another room. One with a candle lit near the center and darkness elsewhere.

"Stands in the middle," his companion ordered.

Hugh did as he was told. An icy feeling crept down his back. His quarry was here, instinct told him as much. Trouble was, was instinct enough to keep him alive for the rest of the night?

The moment the voice spoke, Hugh knew his fears were well founded. It dripped with a quality of evil that was impossible to ignore.

"Who are you?" the voice demanded.

" 'Oo wants to know?" Hugh countered. He allowed a touch of seeming fear to creep into his voice on the last word and then he waited.

"I do," came the answer soft and swift, "and I suggest you answer."

"Oim no'un," Hugh said sullenly, as though cowed and not wanting to be. "Some'un wot wants to live better'n 'is means, is all."

A chuckle. "Well put," came the reply. "Very well, so you've no name. Suits me, as I've no name either."

Hugh straightened up and put a grin on his face as thought he thought he had won. He added a cocky note, this time, as he said, "We could be mates then, roight? You and me? Oi've got oidees, oi do."

Now there was full laughter from the shadows. Hugh could feel the man shake his head. "No, my foolish fellow, we could not be mates. But perhaps you could work for me."

"Woi should oi?" Hugh demanded indignantly.

"Because otherwise," the voice answered amiably, "you will find yourself dead."

Hugh pretended to shrink into himself. "'Ere now, no need for that," he said hastily, frantically. "Oi could works for you, if you loike. Very 'andy oi am wif me fingers. Do well, oi do."

Hugh had the impression of a snake uncoiling before he heard the reply. "Ideas involving Lady Brisbane's household perhaps? Lady Westcott's jewels? Perhaps even the silver?"

Hugh pretended to shrink in upon himself. He started to shake. "'Ow do you know so much?" he asked, the bravado in his voice cracking at the last moment.

A laugh, soft and frightening in the darkness. "I have my sources. Let it be a lesson to you never to underestimate me. You will do as I say or you will die. Is that understood? Do I make myself sufficiently clear?"

"Very clear, guv'nor. Qoite clear," Hugh said hastily. "And oi can be useful, oi can. Woi, just t'day oi took sumfing off a foine gen'lemun, oi did. 'Ere, you can 'as it, you can."

Hugh held out to the man the purse he had taken from Sir Parker's fellow. The one who had brought him seized it from Hugh and passed it over. The man hefted it and seemed to approve.

There was a nod and then silence, as though the person in the shadows was considering what to say or do next. Or perhaps he simply wanted to cow Hugh even further.

At any rate, after several very long moments he said, carelessly, "I think I shall set you a test. I shall have you steal me a bracelet. A bracelet belonging to Lady Westcott. An emerald bracelet. You should have no trouble knowing which one, it is larger than any you will have ever seen, larger than one would think a bracelet should be. You will steal it and bring it tomorrow night. Our friend here will meet you the same place he met you tonight and bring it to where I shall be."

"No." Hugh shook his head. "If oi steals that, oi'll be caught out, oi will. They'll notice straight off and soon think of me. Noi, oi steals only when oi don'ts needs to stay at a place anymore. If you wants me to steal, lets me steal roight. Lets me steal all of the lydie's jewels an' sumfing else besides."

"Ah, so you are not as stupid as you look," the voice said, his amusement patent. "Very well, let me tell you a story. Some time ago, I acquired an emerald bracelet. A bracelet I had wanted for some time. Unfortunately, someone had substituted paste for the real thing. Eventually I discovered that the original owner had sold it to Lord Westcott for his wife. So now you will steal the real bracelet for me and put the false one in its place. If you do it right, no one will ever be the wiser."

Something was tossed and Hugh caught it, clumsily. Still he protested. "Wot if oi can'ts get it by tomorrow noight? It's a very busy 'ouse 'old it is."

"You had better get it by then!" the other hissed. "I don't believe in second chances. Get the bracelet and bring it to the man who brought you here. He shall bring it to me. And don't try to fob me off with the paste one, either, for I shall know the difference at once. Nor can you simply not show up. Wherever you go, wherever you hide, my men will find you. I don't tolerate failures very well. They are likely to end up dead."

"Woi can'ts oi bring it to you meself?" Hugh protested.

"Because the fewer who know how to find me the better. Now go." Then, to the man who had brought Hugh, the voice added sharply, "Take him out the other way."

Hugh shoved the paste bracelet in his pocket. How long had Halifax had it? he wondered. And if he hadn't been in place to steal the real thing, who would Halifax have sent for it?

But there would be time to ponder such matters later. At the moment he had to follow the man who had led him here. As they plunged into darkness and a pathway that led down, Hugh felt a moment of true fear. Was he being led to his death? No, to a tunnel, with water inches deep in the bottom.

Hugh couldn't see a thing and could only conclude that the other man had either memorized the way or was going by touch. Eventually, however, they came out in a cluster of bushes, both men smelling of the noxious fluid they had just come through.

"Go," the other man told him tersely.

"'Ow do oi foinds you tomorrow noight?" he asked.

The other fellow snickered nastily. "Oi don'ts advise trying to foind us. Oi'll foind you, we'll foind you, all right and tight. Just be out on the streets by midnight. Now go! And remember what 'e said: bring that bracelet tomorrow noight or you'll be roight sorry, you will!"

The menace in the other's voice was unmistakable and Hugh hesitated no longer. He began to move quickly away. He had no notion where he was but he kept moving, hoping to find a familiar landmark.

It was later, much later, when he finally rapped at the door in Mayfair. These men seemed to have an inordinate interest in the streetsweep/thief Hugh pretended to be and he had to retire to Lady Brisbane's townhouse and then venture out again, a little later, before he could shake the men following him.

"Good lord!" Sir Parker said as he opened the door to Rowland and the smell reached his nose. "What the devil happened to you?"

Hugh grinned jauntily. "I've been to see the man we're after. At least," he added slowly, "I think I have."

"Well, what did he look like? Did you recognize him?" Parker demanded. "Was it Halifax?"

Hugh shook his head. "I can't be certain. He sat in darkness and his voice was muffled by the hood he wore. The only candle was set near me and I don't think it was a coincidence. But I'm part of the ring now. Loosely part of the ring," he amended. "I've been given my first job—to steal a bracelet from Lady Westcott."

He repeated the story that had been told to him.

"Do you mean to do as he says?" Parker asked sharply.

"I must."

Sir Parker raised his eyebrows but didn't protest. He understood too well what was at stake. "If it is Halifax," he said slowly, "he will give it to Lady Tarren. He has an assignation with her the night of his sister's ball."

Hugh did not ask how Sir Parker knew. He had come to expect this sort of thing from him. He appeared somewhat distracted, however, and Hugh grinned. "Is something wrong?" he asked innocently.

Parker decided to throw tact to the winds. "Oh, the devil with it!" he exclaimed. "You need a bath."

Hugh couldn't help himself, he started laughing.

He might not have been so pleased had he seen Lord Halifax, across town, seated at his desk. There was a puzzled look on his lordship's face. Something about the streetsweeping vagabond had seemed just the slightest bit familiar. He wondered what it was. Had he encountered the man before? That seemed unlikely.

Eventually, just before he blew out the candles in his study and sought his bed, Halifax decided the vagabond must be the by-blow of someone he knew and resembled the fellow a little too closely. In any event, he was not one to trouble himself unduly.

If this streetsweep, pickpocket, and would-be thief proved reliable, it would be very useful to have such a man in Lady Brisbane's household. If not, well, it would be easy enough to dispose of him. Who, after all, would care what happened to a streetsweeping vagabond?

One other person wondered and worried about Hugh. Rebecca watched from her window as he slipped through the darkness to the back door. She was still awake, listening for his footsteps on the servant stairs, her forehead against the window, when she saw him slip out again.

She was tired, so very tired, but she couldn't go to sleep until he returned. Penelope dreamed in her bed and turned in her sleep and Rebecca wished it were as easy for her.

Why did this man catch her imagination as he did? Was it, as Penelope had suggested, that he was simply one more stray creature she had rescued?

It didn't feel that simple to her.

There. He was back again. She must have slept, sitting upright, for by the sky she could tell hours had passed. Tonight Rebecca did not make the mistake of going down to him. Not after the uproar today. Miss Tibbles had protected her once, Rebecca could not ask her to do so again.

With her finger, Rebecca traced his name on the windowpane. Hugh. And then, finally, when she heard his footsteps on the servants stairs, soft as they were, she slipped off the windowseat and between the sheets of her own bed.

Now, at last, she could sleep.

Chapter 8

Rebecca stepped into the room where Hugh was working. He looked tired. Too tired to hear her soft step or the door as she quietly closed it behind her.

But then he had had no more sleep than she had. Less, for she had at least slept with her head cradled against the windowpane while she waited for him to return last night. Now she meant to find out where he had been. It didn't matter if Miss Tibbles caught her for if she didn't find out the answers she needed, she would have to arrange for Hugh to be dismissed herself.

She watched him for a long moment, the way his hands worked quickly and easily, repairing a cabinet that had been damaged the week before. He studied his work, nodded with satisfaction, and worked on it some more.

What was it, she wondered, that was so different about Hugh? Why did he look so, well, reputable was of course an absurd word. As was handsome. But surely one might say he seemed almost a new man, with his clean-shaven face and all. Except that she thought she had seen him steal from a man's pocket.

Rebecca took a step forward, her hands behind her back, an expression of perfect innocence on her face.

"Hugh?"

He jumped and nearly dropped the tools he held. "What is it, Lady Rebecca?" he said.

Rebecca blinked at him and her jaw fell open. Immediately, he seemed to shrink into himself and became the sullen fellow she was used to seeing about the house. And his voice once more became the harsh gutter voice she was accustomed to hearing.

"Oi've gots work, oi do, m'lydie. Wotcher wants wif me?" he demanded.

She sighed. There was exasperation in her voice as she said, "Oh, Hugh, you were making such progress! Why must you fall back into such awful habits when you speak?"

He jutted out his chin and said, belligerently, "Oi am wots oi am, m'lydie."

Rebecca shook her head as she took another step toward him. "Only if you are satisfied to stay that way, and you know it as well as I. If you applied yourself I am certain you could speak quite well and the other servants would soon cease to roast you."

He didn't answer and, emboldened, Rebecca took another step forward. "Why look at you," she said, encouragingly, "you are clean and look much, much better than when I first found you."

"Oi does, m'lydie?" he replied, startled. Then, with a hint of mischief in his eyes and a hint of a smile, he went on cockily, "But wots if oi don'ts wants to be better?"

Rebecca came to a halt a mere hairsbreadth away from him. She put her hands on her hips and spoke with some asperity. "I am well aware, Hugh, that we have not yet managed to tame that unfortunate half of your nature."

She almost mentioned seeing him pick the man's pocket. But what if she was mistaken? They had been, after all, some distance away. Instead she said, "I know you slipped out of the house last night. It can only have been for deplorable reasons and it must stop or I shall be forced to tell my parents what you are doing."

Rebecca paused, then said coaxingly, "Come, Hugh,

surely you are happy to be here? Surely you do not wish to risk losing your place?"

"May'aps oi don'ts belong 'ere," he said helpfully.

Rebecca began to tap her foot. "You are roasting me, Hugh! You could belong here very easily, if you tried, and I am persuaded it is only a matter of helping you to understand that this is so. And of persuading you that you wish to do so."

His shoulders shook and for a moment Rebecca dared to hope he was crying. That would have been a most encouraging sign, in her opinion. But just as she was about to say so, she realized the man was laughing! Laughing at her, she thought, starting to grow very angry.

"Stop that!" she snapped at him, almost stepping on his toes. "Stop that at once, do you hear me! You will not laugh at me! I am Lady Rebecca and your better and I am trying to help you!"

His grin, which had been growing, to her absolute fury, now abruptly disappeared. "Aye, m'lydie, you is. Oi'm grateful, oi am. Just an 'opeless case is all," he said meekly.

Now her eyes filled with tears. "Oh, no, Hugh, don't say so!" Rebecca protested. She reached up and touched the side of his face. "No one is hopeless, I promise you."

He turned his back on her, spurning her touch, but Rebecca somehow understood that it was because he liked it too much, not that he disliked it at all.

Over his shoulder he said, "You'm very kind, m'lydie."

Rebecca smiled wistfully, but of course he could not see her. Not with his back turned toward her. With a shock, she realized that what she most wanted to do was to rest her cheek against his back! She could not, of course, and instead tried to turn her mind to something else.

She studied the cut of his ill-fitting livery and realized

that the cloth looked rough to the touch. It was the first time it had ever occurred to her to wonder whether the servants liked the clothes they wore. She would not have liked to have this stuff against her own skin. But perhaps he did not care? Perhaps he wore enough underneath that none of it touched bare skin.

And the impropriety of that image made Rebecca blush. Distractedly she looked away, then back, then suddenly she froze. Sticking out of Hugh's pocket, just the slightest, was a hint of green and gold. A green and gold bracelet she knew very well. So she had not been mistaken in thinking him a thief. And now it would touch her family as well.

As though he felt her distress, Hugh whirled around and took a step toward her. "Lady Rebecca, are you all right?" he asked.

But Rebecca scarcely heard him. Her voice was faint, and she felt distinctly lightheaded as she said, "Mama's bracelet. You've stolen Mama's bracelet."

Now he was the one who froze. He stood, the color draining from his face and, perversely, she took strength from that.

Rebecca drew a deep breath, then said, firmly, "Give it to me. I shall put it back."

She held her breath as she waited for his answer.

Hugh stared at her, his head spinning. Without knowing he did so, he fingered the cursed bracelet that had edged its way into sight.

He could not give it to her. If she took it up to her mother's jewelry box, she would discover that there were two bracelets. And this wasn't even the real one. He had to think, and quickly, before she decided to rouse the household to capture a thief.

Hugh took a deep breath, pasted a meek, repentant expression on his face and said, "Please, m'lydie, let me put it back meself. Oi'd feel much better, oi would. Oi shouldn't 'ave taken it, oi know. Please let me put it back and make amends loike."

She hesitated, as though unsure of how far to trust him.

"You could watch me, m'lydie," Hugh urged, "and see that I did it roight."

"But what if we are caught?" she asked, still patently unsure.

His voice still meek and earnest, Hugh said coaxingly, "We wouldn'ts be caught, not if'n you was to be a look-out. Make sure, loike, there was no one about, first. And then oi could put it back. Oi would feel better, m'lydie, oi would, if'n oi was to put it back wif me own two 'ands."

Abruptly, she made up her mind. "Very well, we shall do it your way, Hugh. But mind, you are not to steal anything else in this house or I shall go straight to my father and lay everything before him, no matter how angry he is with me for not telling him straightaway."

Hugh let out his breath, almost unable to believe his good fortune. A perverse devil in him could not help but ask, "Woi, m'lydie? Woi are you 'elpin' me?"

She met his eyes steadily and he could not doubt the genuineness of her emotion as she said, warmly, "I have always thought it grossly unfair that some should be born to wealth and comfort and others to the poorest of hovels. You cannot have had an easy time of it. No wonder you are tempted! But I shall help you not to be tempted anymore!"

Hugh wanted to hug her for her kind heart. He wanted to strangle her for seeing more than she ought. Most of all, he wanted the matter over and done with. He could scarcely believe she was going to provide the answer as to how a substitution could be made.

All went smoothly, far more smoothly than Hugh could have predicted. Lady Rebecca led the way to her

mother's dressing room, ensured that it was empty, then
stood in the doorway and said, "Go on, put it back!"

Hugh hesitated, unable to tell her he hadn't the faintest
clue where in the room the jewelry box was to be found,
when she providentially supplied the answer.

"Hurry, Hugh! Now. I know you are tempted to keep
the bracelet, but it will not do. Mama's jewelry box is
right over there, on her dressing table and you are to put
it back in its velvet case, just as you found it."

"Yes, m'lydie."

Hugh glided silently across the room as though he had
done it before. The box was locked but it took only a moment for someone with his skills to open it. There was
more than one velvet case, but he managed the business
swiftly enough that Lady Rebecca did not realize he had
to check more than one before he found the emeralds.
And then, his back carefully blocking her view, he
switched bracelets and the real one went down the front
of his shirt.

He was about to lock the case again when he paused
and looked at her. As he expected, she came to his side
and he showed her the bracelet, safely tucked into its
case. She nodded and he closed and locked the jewelry
box. Then swiftly they both quit the room and returned to
the room where he had been working.

Once safely there, with the door closed so that they
could not be overheard, she looked at him and said,
earnestly, "There now, don't you feel better, Hugh,
knowing you have done the right thing?"

"Oh, oi does, m'lydie, oi most surely does!" he fervently agreed.

"And you are not to steal anything more, Hugh, while
you are in this house," she persisted.

"Oi won'ts, m'lydie," Hugh agreed solemnly. "At
least, oi won'ts if'n oi can 'elps meself."

"Of course you can help yourself," Rebecca said

briskly. "It only wants a little resolution. And I shall help you. I shall watch you every moment I can and stop you if you start to try to steal something. And surely, very soon, the need to steal will go away!"

There was triumph in her voice and Hugh could not doubt that she meant it. What the devil was he to do now? It would be too much to say he felt panic, but he did swallow hard. He tried to look everywhere but at her eyes.

Lady Rebecca, however, was determined. "I believe in you Hugh, and I mean to help you despite yourself. You won't be able to take a step without my watching you and you won't have a chance to do anything wrong."

The image her words drew in his mind caused Hugh to gape at her, appalled. He had no doubt she meant every word she said.

Before he could recover sufficiently to speak, she nodded and said, "I must go now, but don't worry, I truly can save you from yourself. You simply must learn to trust me."

And then, Lady Rebecca left the room and Hugh sank into the nearest seat. He had the bracelet, but clearly slipping out of the house and back again unseen tonight was going to be far from easy.

Curse the girl for watching from her window last night!

Still, the humor of the situation was irresistible and when Jeffries came to check on Hugh's progress with the cabinet, he found him laughing out loud.

Even the major domo's sharp reproof was not enough to wipe the smile entirely from Hugh's face. He was discovering that Lady Brisbane's household was far more lively, far more interesting, than he could ever have guessed in advance. And Lady Rebecca far more than the demure damsel he had first thought her.

Rowland had no doubt Lord and Lady Westcott would cut up rough if they discovered their daughter had

shielded a supposed thief. Nor would they approve her
making him her latest project. He had a shrewd notion
she'd been told to stay away from him and he was also
certain she had no intention of doing so. After all, hadn't
she promised to keep a close eye on him and save him
from himself?

That prompted another chuckle, and Hugh found himself wondering just what turn her efforts to help him
would take next.

Hours later, Hugh wasn't laughing. He had been waiting on the street corner for some time, and was beginning
to think no one would ever show up, when out of the
darkness appeared the man who had led him last night.

" 'Ave you got it?" the man demanded.

Hugh held the bracelet out to him. "Good. 'E'll be
roight 'appy, 'e will."

The man turned to go. "When will oi sees 'im again?"
Hugh asked roughly.

The man laughed, but there was no mirth in his voice.
"You'll sees 'im when 'e says you'll sees 'im, and not a
moment sooner."

And then the man was gone, leaving Hugh to slip back
inside Lady Brisbane's townhouse. This time, he hoped,
unseen.

But she was waiting near the back door, sitting on the
very barrel he had tripped over a few days before. She
was still dressed for the party she had been to, with a
cloak over her shoulders to ward off the chill night air.

Hugh started at the sight and cursed. He stopped several feet away from her and thrust his hands into his
pockets so that they could not betray him. "You'm
oughtn't to be out 'ere," he said.

"I had to check on my animals," she replied, slipping
off the barrel and coming toward him. "But you, I told

you not to sneak out at night again. That wasn't very nice."

"Mebbe oi'm not very noice," Hugh replied, taking a step backward.

She shook her head. "You think so, but I tell you it is possible to change. All that is wanted is resolution. We have had this conversation before, you know. When will you learn that I do not mean to give up?"

Hugh sighed in exasperation. "You oughtn't be out 'ere, m'lydie."

"Neither should you," she countered. "Oh, Hugh, what is it about you that demands this restlessness? I wish, oh, how I wish I could understand and help you more!"

She was truly distressed. He could see it in her eyes, her face, the very way she held her body. And he couldn't bear the thought that she was so worried over him.

"It will all come about, m'lydie," he said, "I promise you."

She stared at him for a long moment. Then, with a perception that startled and dismayed him, she said, "Do you know, Hugh, I almost think it will."

That was when she truly startled him. Lady Rebecca took three long steps and stood so that the top of her head almost touched his chin.

"This ain'ts wise," Hugh croaked.

Lady Rebecca shook her head. "I don't want to be wise," she countered.

Then, before he could stop her, she laid her head against his breast and he had to pull his hands from his pockets and put his arms around her to keep them both from tumbling to the ground.

" 'Ere now!" Hugh said with alarm. "This sort 'o thing could get me turned orf."

Hugh tried to set Lady Rebecca away from him, but she would not let him. He tried to do it with words.

"You orts to be orf wif some gent of yer own sort. Not som'un loikes me. Oi'm a thief, remember?"

Some of the desperation in his voice seemed to reach her. She sighed and stepped away from Hugh. First one step, and then several. And then she turned away, leaving Hugh with an aching loss in his soul.

Over her shoulder she told him, "You're right, of course. I'm not being fair to you. You're the one who would suffer if my parents or my aunt found out about us. And it is my duty to marry someone of my own class. I understand that, I truly do. It is just . . ."

She paused, and the pain in her voice tore at Hugh. He almost took a step toward her and had to force himself to stop. He had to clench his fists at his side to keep from reaching out for her, from trying to hold her close and soothe away her pain.

Lady Rebecca turned and stared at Hugh and he was very glad he had kept the distance between them. Her eyes seemed to shimmer with tears as she said, "I ought to love or at least wish to marry someone of my own sort, as you put it. But I find I cannot. Is there something wrong with me? Something terribly, horribly wrong with me, that I should care more about you than anyone I ought to know? Oh, Hugh, what is there about you that I cannot resist? What weakness is there in my character that I cannot even try?

"You are a thief, you tell me. And I know it with my very own eyes. My mind tells me I am a fool. My heart refuses to listen to reason. Why, Hugh? Why, despite everything, do I persist in thinking I care for you? Why do I persist in trying to protect you? I know you ought not to have been out tonight. I know I ought to rouse my father from his bed and tell him. But I cannot. What is so wrong with me that I forget my duty, my consequence, every precept of propriety that has ever been taught me?"

Hugh swallowed hard. He had a suspicious shimmer in

his own eyes now. He could not bear to hear her deride herself this way. He ached to tell her that perhaps her instincts were stronger than his disguise. But he could not. Not for her sake, and certainly not for his own.

He did not speak. But this time, when she stepped closer and rested her head on his breast, he did not hesitate either. His arms went around Lady Rebecca to give her what warmth, what little comfort he could.

And when she lifted her face up toward his and asked him to kiss her, he did.

He would hate himself in the morning, Hugh told himself, even as he kissed the corners of her mouth. And no doubt she would hate him as well, he added, as he kissed her eyelids. And no doubt her parents would hate, perhaps kill him, if ever they found out what he had done.

But surely it was not so very horrible a crime? he told himself, as his lips moved to capture softly, sweetly, tenderly hers. He'd never kissed a lady so innocent. All the women he'd known, since Felicity had crushed his faith in love, had been experienced, not likely to misunderstand what he could and couldn't offer. He'd never before taken the chance of raising expectations he couldn't fulfill.

But he wasn't really doing so now. Lady Rebecca would never dream of a future with Hugh, streetsweep and thief. No, he was merely giving a young girl a tiny dream she could hold in her heart and, perhaps, look back upon with affection, through all the days of her life.

And then she said words that shattered *his* fantasy. Words that acted like a bucket of icy cold water on his ardor.

"I love you," Lady Rebecca whispered against his lips.

Instantly, Hugh sprang back. He couldn't let things get this far out of hand. He couldn't let her weave such dreams about the man he pretended to be. Or even the

man he really was. He blinked; he looked about for a way
to escape; he stammered.

"Oi've gots to be going in, m'lydie. And so do you.
You don'ts wants me, m'lydie. And oi," he stopped and
swallowed, for it was far more difficult than he had expected to make himself say the rest of the words, "oi
don'ts wants you."

Chapter 9

Hugh stood in the darkness watching as ladies and gentlemen arrived in their carriages. He was taking a chance by being here, dressed as a guest rather than as the character he was pretending to be. But it was a masquerade, and if Halifax caught him, he could always try to claim he was masquerading as a gentleman to find some pockets to pick.

He wouldn't admit to himself that he wanted the chance to dance, just once, with Lady Rebecca. Now, when she couldn't read more into it than he meant. He told himself instead that he owed it to her to try to discover Halifax's intentions toward her. And toward Lady Penelope.

Briefly he wondered if Halifax's mistress, Lady Tarren, would be here and if she was, how Halifax would juggle his interest in all three. But no, he decided. Lady Tarren, a lady by birth, a courtesan by choice, was snubbed by every respectable hostess in London. She wouldn't have an invitation.

As for Hugh, he had no intention of pressing his luck by entering through the front door. Not when there were plenty of shadows to hide in as he slipped round the back way. French doors stood open from the ballroom onto balconies, and it was no trick for Hugh to climb up to one of them. Though he did have to hang below it a trifle longer than he liked when a couple came out upon his chosen balcony unexpectedly.

But then someone called the couple back inside and in a trice Hugh was up on the balcony, brushing off his evening clothes and drawing his black domino close about himself. His mask was in place and, taking a deep breath, he stepped inside the ballroom.

Rebecca felt as though she had stepped into a book of some magical tale as one gentleman after another danced with her. It was not her first ball this Season, but it was her first masquerade. She laughed, she flirted, she drank the glasses of lemonade gentlemen procured for her.

Mama watched it all with approval. If Mama gave a tiny frown occasionally, Rebecca dismissed it as unimportant. She had been told to charm the gentlemen and she was doing her best, wasn't she? Was it her fault that Penelope refused to dance and instead sat there glowering at any gentleman who dared to approach? It was not as if Rebecca had any power to cause Penelope to behave any differently. Besides, it seemed to fascinate the gentlemen, and several clustered around her twin persistently.

And then the musicians struck up a waltz. Even without Mama's frantic signal, Rebecca would have known she wasn't allowed to dance it. Not before she had been to Almack's and received approval from one of the patronesses. But how to get out of the way of the dancers and back around to Mama? Her current cavalier had gone to get her yet another glass of lemonade.

Rebecca smiled despite herself. It had been, after all, a very effective way to get rid of the impertinent fellow. Suddenly a gentleman stood next to her. Rebecca started, for she hadn't seen him coming.

"May I have this dance?" he asked, bowing low.

Rebecca was tired, but she made herself smile as she shook her head and said, "I am very sorry, sir, but you must know that I have not yet been given permission."

He bowed again. "I am very sorry to hear it," he said meekly. "I did not know."

Rebecca's eyes narrowed. His voice seemed oddly familiar, she thought, but who was he? Not any of the young men she had already danced with tonight. Nor any she had met who had courted her sisters. Therefore she ought not to encourage him. Rebecca waited for the stranger to go away.

But he didn't go away. Instead, he had the impertinence to suggest, "Perhaps we could sit and talk?"

She hesitated. She wished she could recall where she had heard his voice before. But she could not. And if she had not been introduced to him properly, she ought to refuse. And yet, this was a masquerade. She could always pretend she thought she had known him. Besides, beneath his mask, she had the impression this stranger was ill at ease, perhaps even a little forlorn. Perhaps she should take him under her wing, Rebecca thought brightly. Certainly she could not bear to crush him entirely.

She shook her head and said, "But you could take me back to my mother. That would be unexceptionable."

It was his turn to hesitate. But then he offered her his arm and Rebecca took it. They were only halfway to Lady Westcott and Lady Brisbane, however, when another gentleman stopped them by stepping straight into their path. Her escort would have gone around the man, but Rebecca knew better. She stopped and waited for him to speak.

"You are very lovely tonight, m'lady," the man's rich warm voice told her as he bowed to Rebecca.

"Lord Halifax!" she exclaimed, recognizing his voice with pleasure. "I had wondered where you were. I thought perhaps you hadn't come."

Halifax put a hand over his chest as though wounded. "Not come to my own sister's ball? What sort of a cad do you take me for?"

"A very theatrical one," Rebecca's companion muttered.

Halifax shot the man a sharp look. "And who is this?" he asked Rebecca.

She colored. She dared not admit she didn't know. Mama would be furious with her. To be sure, it was not as improper as it would be at an ordinary ball, but Rebecca was quite sure that Mama would say a girl could never be too careful of her reputation.

The gentleman came to her rescue. "An old family friend," he said lightly, "presuming to escort the young lady back to her mother."

"Ah, but I have not yet had the chance to talk with her this evening. Please let me escort her back," Halifax countered smoothly.

Rebecca had the distinct impression Halifax did not care whether he escorted her back to her mother, that he only wished to discompose the stranger. But the stranger appeared not to care. He bowed and started to retreat, leaving Halifax to offer Rebecca his arm. She was not altogether pleased to take it.

As the stranger moved past Halifax, he seemed to stumble, but promptly righted himself and apologized. So she had been right, Rebecca thought with compassion, the poor fellow did feel out of place. She really wished she had been able to set him at his ease.

Outside, in the hallway, Hugh silently cursed his luck. He had had no chance to dance with Lady Rebecca, nor was he pleased to have had to hand her over to Halifax. But he dared not risk being unmasked by drawing Halifax into a dispute in the ballroom.

Still, it was not all a loss. Hugh smiled. In his pocket was the bracelet Halifax had intended to give to Lady Tarren. Lady Westcott's bracelet. He had retrieved it when he clumsily bumped into Halifax.

Not that he should have taken the risk. But Hugh could not resist seeing if Halifax had it on his person. Besides, the notion that it would end up on the arm of one of the most notorious women in London, even if she was a lady, displeased him. He would far rather set it in a safe place and know that when this was all over he would be returning it to Lady Westcott.

Rowland waited a few more minutes, then headed back inside the ballroom. He found Lady Rebecca immediately. It was as though there were some invisible link between them, drawing his eyes to wherever she might be.

Now she was dancing. And not with Halifax. Hugh let out the breath he didn't realize he was holding. He also spared a glance for Lady Penelope. The poor girl looked most uncomfortable. He wished there was something he could do that would make it easier for her, but he feared there wasn't. For one thing, he was a member of that dreaded species she hated—men. Like everyone else in the Brisbane household, he knew her views.

Second, her mother would never allow him to speak to the girl without a proper introduction and he couldn't tell her, couldn't tell anyone, who he was. In fact, he would have to be extremely careful to be out of here before the official unmasking.

And then Hugh saw Sir Parker. There was no mistaking the man, for he hadn't bothered with the nonsense of a mask and domino. His figure was rotund, his clothes elegant, and he was in earnest conversation with a number of men, including Lord Westcott. Hugh slipped closer so that he could overhear.

Sir Parker was playing, admirably, the role he did so well—that of wealthy buffoon. There were very few people in England who knew how shrewd a mind he truly had. Rowland was one of them.

"Really, a most extraordinary piece. I think my mother will like it. She should. It's worth a king's ransom," Sir Parker was saying. "And a matching parure."

Hugh suppressed an unholy grin. Sir Parker was setting

out bait. And to that end, he was here to let all and sundry know about the supposed jewelry.

Hugh watched for signs that anyone was listening with particular interest to Sir Parker's description of what he was supposedly about to buy for his mother. Several gentlemen were intent upon his description. One of them was Halifax.

When the talk turned to other matters, Rowland silently slipped away to watch again as Lady Rebecca danced. He should have been reassured that she was so popular tonight, giving Halifax no chance to monopolize her attentions. Instead, Hugh found he had an oddly bereft sensation as he watched, knowing that he could not risk taking a turn after all. Not when Halifax had already shown too great an interest in his presence here.

Finally, when he could stand it no longer, Rowland slipped away for the final time. Sir Parker was calling for his cloak and with a grin, Hugh decided to surprise him. They needed to talk. Silently he left the house and went to find Sir Parker's carriage.

Sometime later, Lady Brisbane and Lady Westcott chattered happily as their carriage headed back home. Penelope and Rebecca exchanged looks of amusement, though there was an edge to Penelope's smile that worried her twin.

Still, the evening had been a success. Even Penelope had to acknowledge that there was something gratifying about the fact that the gentlemen she had met were, for the most part, undeterred by her attempts to drive them away. Not that she wished for their attentions, of course, but nevertheless it was gratifying that they sought out her company. For after all, she admitted aloud, one could have friends who were men, so long as everyone understood she would never marry.

Lady Westcott and Lady Brisbane exchanged knowing glances at this declaration, but neither felt equal to disputing it at such a late hour. Or perhaps one should say such an early hour, for it was closer to dawn than to midnight.

Each of the ladies yawned, however indelicate that might be, as the footman handed her out of the carriage. Each one protested how eager she was to find her bed.

Perhaps their fatigue was the reason that only Rebecca noticed the figure who slipped through the bushes toward the back of the house. She frowned. It must be Hugh, despite her efforts to reform him.

Not for the first time she struggled with the thought that she ought to warn her aunt and Papa about him. But how could she? She was certain she could save Hugh, but if she told them what she knew, they would give her no chance to do so.

With a sigh, Rebecca realized she would have to speak very sternly to Hugh again in the morning.

A little earlier, across town, Lord Halifax mounted the steps to the jewel of a townhouse where Lady Tarren lived. He smiled to himself with anticipation.

Lady Tarren's major domo opened the door to Halifax and greeted him by saying, "She is waiting for you upstairs, m'lord."

Thank you. I shall show myself up."

"Of course, m'lord."

Lady Tarren was indeed waiting in her bedroom. Tonight she had outdone herself. The room looked as though it were part of some Turkish harem. And she had, from somewhere, conjured up an appropriately matching costume.

The costume left very little, indeed nothing, to the imagination. Wispy veils revealed far more than they concealed and the girdle that held them up was scarcely wider than a finger's width anywhere around.

Halifax swallowed hard and took a step into the room, closing the door behind him even though he knew none of her servants would dare disturb them.

"You look so ravishing tonight," he said hoarsely.

She beamed at him. "That was the point. But come over here and show me just how much you appreciate all this," Lady Tarren added, crooking her finger to beckon him.

Halifax needed no second urging. When he reached the side of the bed and reached for her, Lady Tarren held up a hand to forestall him.

"My present?" she asked softly.

"Of course," Halifax purred. "I have it right here in my pocket."

Thinking of the pleasure ahead, Halifax dipped his fingers into the pocket where he had placed the bracelet he meant to give her. And cursed as his fingers came up empty.

Lady Tarren sat upright. Her eyes narrowed. "Is something wrong, Halifax?" she demanded, no longer quite so sultry in her tones.

"No, no, of course not," Halifax replied hastily as he searched his other pockets. "I know I have your present here somewhere. It is only a matter of finding it."

Her eyes narrowed further. Her lips pressed into a hard, thin line. There was not the least trace of sympathetic understanding in her expression.

Indeed one might almost have said she expected it when Halifax lifted his head, looked at her with a stricken expression on his face, and said, "I must have lost it somewhere. But I swear you would have loved it! A bracelet of emeralds. To match your emerald eyes."

Lady Tarren swung her feet over the side of the bed and reached for a robe that would cover her from chin to toe. "Of course," she said in a brittle voice.

"No, really," Halifax protested.

She turned and faced him. "Really? Then get me another one."

His face fell. "I cannot," he confessed. "It was one of a kind. I'm not even certain there is anyone who can make another. Certainly not without a copy before him."

Now Lady Tarren's eyes blazed with anger. The heavy, almost overpowering scent of patchouli filled the room, released by the rising heat of her body.

"You promised me that bracelet and you said you would have it for me tonight. Well, I want it. Don't come back here until you bring it with you."

"Be reasonable," Halifax protested, spreading his hands wide. "I have told you it was one of a kind. Let me bring you something else. Something much better."

Lady Tarren stopped and turned and looked at him thoughtfully. "Better?" she echoed.

Halifax nodded vigorously.

"How better?" she demanded.

He thought rapidly and then remembered Sir Parker. Halifax described the piece as he remembered Sir Parker describing it. When he was done, he held his breath and watched Lady Tarren's face.

For a long moment, matters hung in the balance. Then she nodded grudgingly. "Perhaps it would do," she conceded. "Very well, when you have that piece you may bring it to me and," she added purring, "I shall make you very happy when I show you my gratitude."

Halifax swallowed hard as she allowed her robe to fall open again. "It may take a few days," he warned.

Lady Tarren snapped shut the robe and tied it. "You have one week" she hissed. "Then I shall find someone else to amuse and who will amuse me. And value me as I deserve. One week, Halifax."

Hastily he rose to his feet, his face pale. "Yes, of course. I promise I shall have it for you by then."

Lady Tarren merely smiled and watched as Halifax all but ran out of the room. It was so amusing watching men make fools of themselves over her. Still, it was strange, she thought, her smile turning to a frown, that he did not have the bracelet.

She rose and moved to the writing desk on the far side of

the room. It only took a few minutes to write a note, fold and seal it. Another to ring for a servant and give orders for the note to be delivered at once.

And then Lady Tarren sat at her desk thinking. She was, she realized, very tired of the life she was leading. There was a time when she had thought it fun. But that was long ago. And yet, she could see no way out, no way to go back to the innocent girl she once had been.

But it was all foolishness, she told herself. She was doing what she had to do, what it was important to do. It was useless to think of anything else.

With a tiny sigh, Lady Tarren blew out the candles and slowly climbed back into bed.

Halifax sat in a corner of one of the most infamous gaming hells in London. Tonight the play at the tables gave him no pleasure. He found his mind turning again and again to the question of the bracelet. He had had it when he set out for his sister's ball, of that he was certain. It must have been lost there.

Lost or taken? That was the question. But who would dare to steal it from him? And when and how?

Halifax's mind kept turning to the stranger at the ball who had stumbled against him. He knew the man's voice, he would swear it, and yet he could not say how.

Abruptly a notion occurred to him and he sat up very straight. Impossible! And yet, was it? The man who had stolen the bracelet for Halifax had already proven himself unusual and resourceful, why not consider this? Could he have successfully masqueraded as a gentleman?

And if he had, what then? Punish him? Or use him? Halifax idly rubbed his chin as he pondered the matter. If only he could be certain.

Perhaps it was time to summon the man to him again. There was a task that could be set which would be an even better test than the one before. If he failed, why then he would be disposed of. If he succeeded, then he would be bound to them all.

But perhaps it would be best if Halifax did not see him again until after he had been tested. One did not wish to give the man a chance to recognize him. There would be time enough to bring the man directly before him when he had done what Halifax wished. When he was bound to them by ties that could not be broken.

Slowly, a very malevolent smile spread across Halifax's face. He began to rise to his feet to go and arrange everything, but then he sat back down again. Perhaps it would be best to wait a few days, let the man think he had gone undetected. Then, when he felt most secure, let him be summoned and told what he was to do.

With far more energy than he had shown thus far, Halifax began to gamble.

Chapter 10

Rebecca went looking for Hugh early, wanting to speak to him before the rest of her family was up and about. He was polishing silver and she felt a moment of panic. What if he found he could not resist the temptation? It would be so easy, after all, to slip a spoon or two into his pockets.

She would have to speak to Jeffries, Rebecca decided, about giving Hugh a safer task as soon as possible. But right now, she was determined to speak to Hugh herself.

He must have been very absorbed in his task, for when she gently touched his arm, he almost dropped the silver he was holding.

"Wot the devil? M'lydie! Wot are you going in 'ere? You shouldn't be 'anging around the loikes o' me." he said sternly.

Rebecca supposed the harshness in his voice was meant to shove her away, but she couldn't believe in it. Not when he was also looking at her with such a glow in his eyes, as though she brightened his day simply by being there. Which was, she told herself sternly, a very fanciful and improbable thought. Her heart refused to listen.

"It's all right," Rebecca assured him soothingly, "no one can overhear us. I made certain of that before I came in here. But I must speak to you."

"Oh?" he asked warily.

Rebecca sighed and made herself speak firmly. "I know

you were out again last night. I thought it was understood there was to be no more of that nonsense!"

He lowered his head and his expression was meek, but Rebecca had the oddest notion he was laughing at her as he said, in a hopeful voice, "P'rhaps you saw some'un else, m'lydie?"

"I know what I saw," she replied tartly. "You were sneaking in the back way just as my mother and aunt and sister and I were getting home."

"Oh."

"You don't deny it?" she asked, nonplused.

He scratched the side of his nose and his voice was earnest, but with the intonations of someone telling a fanciful story, rather than the truth.

"It's loike this, m'lydie. Oi gets feverish loike if oi 'as ter stay inside too long. Oi needs to get out and stretch me legs a bit, oi do."

"In the early hours of the morning, I suppose?" Rebecca suggested helpfully.

"That's it," he agreed. "Dead on, m'lydie. Roight near dawn oi gets restless."

"And near midnight?"

"Oh, powerful restless, then," he agreed.

Rebecca threw up her hands. "You are hopeless!" she said impatiently. "You have no intention of telling me the truth, do you?"

"No," he cheerfully agreed.

She put her hand on his arm again. "Oh, Hugh, why must you do this?" she asked softly. "You know that if you do not reform, then sooner or later I must tell my aunt and my parents about you."

He put his hand over hers and his voice was soft and low as he said, earnestly, "Soon, m'lady, soon I may be able to tell you all."

Rebecca stared at him. Had her ears deceived her? For

the veriest of moments he had spoken like a gentleman, no
hint of the streets in his voice.

But no, she must have been mistaken, for the coarseness
was there, as broad as ever, as he said, pulling his hand
abruptly away from hers, "Oi'd best be getting back to me
work, m'lydie."

Rebecca yanked her hand free, pursed her lips, then
whirled around and stalked from the room. At the doorway
she paused to warn him.

"I shall hold you to your promise to tell me the truth
soon," she said. "Otherwise, I shall tell my parents everything."

Rebecca's interest in Hugh did not go unnoticed. Lady
Brisbane was all too well aware of the way she followed
him about. A direct application to the girl, however,
brought a forthright statement that she had indeed been following the man. Because she intended to help him.

"That is quite admirable," Lady Brisbane began.

"Oh, I am so glad you think so!" Rebecca said, hugging
her before her aunt could finish her sentence. "I was so
afraid, you see, that you would be so stodgy as to forbid me
to do so."

Well, if there was one thing Lady Brisbane was not, it
was stodgy. Recognizing impossible terrain when she saw
it, her ladyship retreated and prepared to call in the residual
forces. First she spoke to Miss Tibbles. It was only natural
that they should form an alliance to deal with the matter.

"Do you think we should be concerned?" Lady Brisbane
asked the governess bluntly, in the privacy of her own sitting room.

Miss Tibbles hesitated, then began to speak frankly. "I
am not certain. I have tried to keep a close rein upon the
girl, but too tight a rein and we shall truly be in the suds."

Lady Brisbane nodded vigorously. "Just so. Rebecca is a
Westcott girl. However meek she generally seems, she will

not brook opposition. And heaven forbid my sister or her husband should discover what is afoot or they will make a mess of everything. I wonder, however, if perhaps one of her sisters might be of use here. What does Penelope tell you?"

"Nothing," Miss Tibbles answered bluntly.

Lady Brisbane shifted in her chair, betraying her agitation. "Well, I cannot like it that he is always hanging about her! Or perhaps it is the other way around. She is always hanging about him."

Miss Tibbles colored, then cleared her throat and said cautiously, "Some of that is perhaps my fault. I thought it perhaps a good notion to have a strong, devoted servant accompany her whenever she goes out."

Lady Brisbane stared at Miss Tibbles. Several times she seemed to start to speak and then stopped herself. Miss Tibbles had that effect upon people. After a moment she did manage to ask, in a somewhat strangled voice, "What do you suggest, then, Miss Tibbles?"

The governess smiled thinly. "I have been thinking of her sisters. There might be a possibility that she would tell them what is going on and allow them to guide her."

Both ladies were silent as they pictured Rebecca's sisters. "Perhaps not Barbara," Lady Brisbane said cautiously. "Or Diana."

Miss Tibbles nodded. "I was thinking of Annabelle. They used to be close and she was always a dutiful child. Perhaps she can talk to Rebecca and help her to recollect her position."

"Perfect!" Lady Brisbane agreed. She would waste no time in arranging everything.

So it was that a few days later, Rebecca entered the drawing room warily. There was no knowing who might have come to call today. It was as though she had gone from being all but invisible, to the toast of the *ton*, overnight. And even Penelope had her admirers.

In particular, every day a cluster of young gentlemen came to call. And while it was most flattering, and even amusing at first, the unlooked-for attention began to wear upon Rebecca. And Penelope. Each day as the gentlemen came, she grew more and more upset about the matter.

So now, told that she was wanted in the drawing room, that she had a caller, Rebecca opened the door to it with a tremulous sensation in the pit of her stomach. And felt an instant sense of relief that was immediately replaced by an even greater sense of wariness as she spied Annabelle. Particularly as her sister was watching her reprovingly.

Rebecca advanced, knowing an attempted retreat would be fatal. "Oh, no, you don't!" she said. "You are not going to scold me! I am only trying to help a poor, unfortunate fellow I found on the street who saved my life. And if we are going to talk about propriety—"

Before Rebecca could complete the words, Annabelle spoke out. "Don't you dare repeat that gossip about Winsborough and me! It is precisely what gives me the right to counsel you now."

"Oh?"

Annabelle tried to placate her. "Dearest, you know we are only concerned about you," she said. "And so is Aunt Ariana. And Miss Tibbles."

Rebecca began to pace with some agitation. "There is no need to be concerned," she said. "I am not likely to lose my head and do something foolish."

"I collect you have already done something foolish," Annabelle countered dryly. "You brought home a man you found in the streets."

Rebecca rounded on her sister. "He saved my life! What was I supposed to do? Walk away without expressing my gratitude?"

"No, of course not," Annabelle said at once. "It is only

that Aunt Ariana and Miss Tibbles worry that you are too concerned about the fellow still."

Rebecca stared at the floor. Concerned about him? Of course she was! And always would be.

"Aren't there any of your suitors you like enough to let one divert you?" Annabelle asked, a hint of desperation in her voice.

Rebecca made herself smile brightly. "Oh, many. And they do divert me. I vow I have never laughed so much as I have this past week. Why, just yesterday Lord Halifax . . ."

Outside the drawing room, Hugh leaned his head against the door and listened. It seemed to be only female voices. Good. Halifax had not come to call. Or any other gentlemen, for that matter.

Hugh knew he ought to be happy for Lady Rebecca, that she was well on her way to finding a gentleman who would come up to scratch, who would offer to marry her. But he wasn't. The notion made him feel distinctly ill.

Which was absurd. Once this job was over, he would never see her again. He ought to be grateful his presence meant so little to her. Indeed, he should have been more afraid that she would dog his heels, fancying herself in love with him. After all, with the example of his parents and his older brother before him, Hugh ought to be glad to walk so easily away from the girl.

And yet, oddly, he wasn't. He found himself almost wishing he could court Lady Rebecca. He found himself, from time to time, wondering what it would be like to come home to her. Which was ridiculous. Had he learned nothing from Felicity? He had thought she was kind. He had thought she was as sweet and innocent as Lady Rebecca. If he had been so wrong once, who was to say he was not wrong again now?

"Hugh! What the devil are you doing there?"

Hugh turned to face Lady Brisbane advancing upon him,

fury written upon her face. He went pale. So pale that her fury turned to patent concern.

"Are you unwell?" she asked. "You look about to faint. Go down to cook and have her give you a strong cup of tea. Then lie down on your bed and rest for an hour or two. If Jeffries objects, tell him I told you to do so."

"Yes, m'lydie."

Hastily, he started for the servants stairwell. Lady Brisbane's cool voice stopped him as she said, "And Hugh?"

"Yes, m'lydie?"

"Don't ever let me catch you listening at doorways again."

"No, m'lydie!"

Hugh hurried away before she could ask or tell him anything more. He didn't know why he hadn't been dismissed on the spot, but whatever the reason, he was grateful. How the devil could he have been so careless?

It was because the Duke of Berenford had once masqueraded as a groom in the Westcott household and won the heart of the eldest daughter, Diana, that Rowland had not been dismissed. Not that anyone really expected the same sort of thing to ever happen again, but still, it added just a note of caution to the way the family dealt with their servants. It accounted for his luck at the moment, though there were distinct limits to how far that luck could be pressed.

Downstairs in the kitchens, Cook was happy to give Hugh a cup of tea and fuss over him. Jeffries would have sent him back to his work but when he repeated what Lady Brisbane had said, the major domo pressed his lips into a thin line but did not countermand the orders.

Hugh had just begun to relax when disaster struck. Miss Tibbles entered the kitchens, looked around, then fixed her eyes grimly upon him.

"You," she said. "I wish to speak with you. Come take a turn in the garden with me."

Hugh had no choice but to follow, albeit very warily.

Outside, Miss Tibbles wasted no time. "This must stop, Hugh!" she said.

"Wot?" he countered, feeling his ground.

"I am well aware that Lady Rebecca harbors entirely unacceptable feelings toward you," Miss Tibbles said frankly. "And now I discover you have been listening at doors?"

How the devil was he to explain that? She would not be fobbed off as easily as the others in this household. In the end, he did what he had always done when cornered. He told the truth. Insofar as it would serve him, that is.

"Oi wanted to be sure 'er lydieship weren't talking wif Lord 'alifax," Hugh said, fixing earnest, wide-open eyes on the governess's face. "Oi don'ts trust 'im, oi don'ts."

For a moment he thought he had persuaded her. Then she started to tap her foot, a sure sign of impatience. "Neither do I, but I don't listen at doorways," she said, with some asperity.

Hugh grinned. He couldn't help himself. "You don'ts 'as to," he said. "You could be in the room. Me, oi doesn't 'as no choice."

She continued to stare at him with her sharp, piercing eyes. "Now why," she said thoughtfully, "don't I quite believe you, I wonder?"

"Oi only wants wots best for 'er," Hugh said, still in the same earnest voice as before.

Miss Tibbles frowned. "I know you are telling me the truth about that," she said, not troubling to hide her confusion. "I simply don't understand why you care. You cannot be so foolish as to dismiss the difference in your stations."

Rarely had Hugh regretted the need for deception more than now. Reluctantly, awkwardly, he tried to explain in a way that would not betray his masquerade. "She 'elped me, Lydie Rebecca did. Oi wouldn't wants nuffing to 'appen to 'er. No'un's 'elped me before."

Even as he said it, Hugh realized it was the truth. For years he had helped his country—done whatever was asked of him, undertaken any sort of masquerade. And before that he had taken care of his mother and brother after his father died. Until she died as well and his brother married. There had been money, a great deal of it, but not much love or concern for him. He had been someone to help his brother, the heir, to carry on the family name.

No one had ever worried over Hugh as Lady Rebecca did, and he found it mattered much more to him than he could ever have guessed beforehand.

Some of this must have shown in his face, for Miss Tibbles slowly nodded. "It is an excellent thing you feel as you do," she said. "When Lady Rebecca gives her sympathy, whether to an injured bird or squirrel or cat or even to a vagabond, she gives it completely. It would hurt her greatly if you were to betray her trust."

Hugh looked at Miss Tibbles and answered solemnly. It was as though they made a pact between them. "Oi can'ts 'elp if things moight look wrong, some'ow. But oi swears, it will all work out. Oi wouldn'ts do nuffing to 'urt 'er."

"Oddly enough," she said again, "I believe you."

And then, against all odds, they smiled at one another. Rebecca, watching from an upstairs window, could only shake her head in wonder.

Chapter 11

The note came to Hugh as he was cleaning out the coal shuttle. No one could say who had delivered it, just that it had come for him.

He made certain he was alone before he unscrewed it and read what was written there. He was being summoned. Tonight. And there was a warning not to fail.

Because he could not know if this meant Halifax had recognized him the night of the ball, he was doubly careful to be there when Halifax came to call with some other gentlemen. Hugh stayed out of sight, of course, but he managed to be near the foyer when Halifax took his leave and he saw a coin pass between the man and Jeffries, as well as several words. Still, he didn't look as though he were certain of anything.

Hugh also accompanied Lady Rebecca and her sister and their governess when the three took a walk to the nearby park. He carried shawls and parasols, in case they should be needed. He also kept watch for any strangers observing them. But all he saw was Damian, Lord Farrington, with Lady Farrington, and that alone was almost enough to have him undone.

They were in the middle of the park when a carriage drew to a halt nearby and a lady jumped down, coming swiftly toward the walking party. Lord Farrington handed the reins to his groom and slowly followed.

"Penelope! Rebecca! Miss Tibbles! How delightful to see you!" the lady cried as she ran up to them.

"Lady Farrington!" Miss Tibbles said warningly.

But the girls all ignored her. "Barbara! You are back from the country! How delightful to see you. And what nice cattle," Lady Rebecca said with approval.

Lady Farrington laughed. "Yes, they are nice goers, aren't they. And you? Found beaux, have you?"

"I don't want a beau. I shan't ever marry," Lady Penelope pronounced with a definite sniff. "And neither shall Rebecca. We have made a pact between us."

Rebecca was more shy, avoiding her sister's shrewd eyes. "Surely there is no hurry," she said naively.

By this time Farrington had come up behind his wife and placed a hand lightly around her waist as he greeted his wife's family. Then, over the top of their heads, he spotted Hugh and his eyes narrowed.

Hugh knew the precise moment that Farrington recognized him, blast his perceptive eyes! He cocked his head in an unspoken question and Hugh gave the tiniest shake of his own head. Immediately, Farrington took the hint and looked away, pretending his interest fixed on a point in Hugh's direction but much farther away.

Farrington was a good man and would not betray him. Still, Rowland was relieved when the Farringtons took their leave of the Westcott party and returned to their carriage. After this was over, Farrington would no doubt call on him for an accounting, but, for the moment at least, the danger was past.

Hugh followed the Westcott girls and their governess back to the household. More than ever, he wished this latest assignment was over. He had almost finished the box he was making for Lady Rebecca's cat and her kittens, and he meant to leave it for her when he went.

As for Farrington, he made himself a mental note to go around to visit his wife's family and try to have a quiet word with Hugh. If that were not possible, he ought to at least see if he could discreetly discover from Lord Westcott what his old friend was doing here.

It was a lively household that evening, what with the Farringtons coming over for a family dinner, standing upon no ceremony once the Westcotts discovered they were in town and promptly invited them. When they were all safely ensconced in the drawing room, happily gossiping with one another, Damian made an excuse to go out for a few minutes to, as he said, blow a cloud.

"Smoking? Disgusting habit!" Lady Brisbane proclaimed disapprovingly.

Farrington disarmed her with a disingenuous smile and swore not to return to the drawing room until the smell of the smoke had left him. He carefully did not meet his wife's eyes, for he knew Barbara would be watching him, knowing something was afoot.

He did not smoke, of course, but it was an excellent excuse to make his way out to the back yard. There, as he expected, Hugh soon slipped out to meet him.

"Odd rig you seem to be running," Damian said without preamble. "Shouldn't think there would be anything havey-cavey in this household needing your attention."

"There isn't."

"Then why are you here? Lord Westcott gave me some ridiculous story that you were a streetsweep who saved Lady Rebecca's life."

Hugh smiled. "I did. It was an accident, but a rather fortuitous one. Since then I have stolen Lady Westcott's bracelet, picked some pockets, and soon I shall probably do far worse."

Instead of recoiling in shock, Farrington quirked an eyebrow. "Have you now? It sounds like fun. Anything I can help with?"

Hugh considered the offer seriously. Farrington was a good man to have in one's corner. They had worked together before. Regretfully, however, he discarded the notion. Sir Parker, and indeed Hugh himself, had a distinct prejudice against using men who were married. They risked too much. Not just for themselves, but for the ones they loved. Still, he was a good man to have in reserve.

So now he shook his head. "Not at the moment, but I may call upon you without warning, if need be."

Farrington nodded. They were silent together for some moments, then he said, "Can you tell me about it?"

"No."

"Will it be over soon?"

Hugh shrugged.

"Grown loquacious, have you, since the Peninsula?" Farrington suggested tartly.

Hugh grinned. "I don't know, and that's the truth. I have some hope it will be settled soon, but no guarantees. And when it is settled, there is likely to be quite a dust-up over who gets caught."

Farrington nodded. "If I can help, let me know. If not, well, when it is over, I shall expect you to come around and tell me all about it."

"I shall."

Neither Rebecca nor Penelope was thinking about Lord Farrington and Hugh. At least not together. But after the Farringtons had left and the girls were in bed, Rebecca said softly, in the darkness, "Do you think Barbara looked happy, Penelope?"

"Disgustingly happy," Penelope replied.

Rebecca smiled, knowing her sister could not see her face. "Why do you say it so?" she asked.

"Because she has lost all sense of who she is!" Penelope said hotly. "She is not the same Barbara she was before."

"No," Rebecca agreed thoughtfully, "she is not. But I think she is better for it."

"Oh, there is no talking to you!" Penelope exclaimed.

Rebecca did not try to answer that charge. After several moments, Penelope said softly, "Do you think you will ever change your mind, Rebecca, and marry?"

She hesitated, and Penelope went on, "It's all right. I know I have said to everyone that we both swore we would not, but if you truly wished to do so, I would understand."

"No you wouldn't," Rebecca countered with a grin.

"Well, no," Penelope admitted. "But I would try to be happy for you. Is there someone you've a *tendre* for?"

Rebecca took a very long time to answer. "Yes," she said slowly, "but he can never marry me."

"Hugh."

It was not a question, it was a name whispered softly, full of understanding of what such a thing meant.

"Yes, Hugh," Rebecca agreed, just as softly. "I know it is nonsense, but there is something about the man that draws me to him. He needs me, Penelope."

"I am not certain that is a good or sufficient basis for marriage," her sister answered cautiously.

"I know." Rebecca rose from her bed and went to stand by the window. She leaned her forehead against the pane as she said, "I also need him. His strength. His laughter, though I see it only in his eyes, for he does not laugh aloud. The quickness of his hands. The spark of caring I see in his eyes when he looks at me and even at my animals when he thinks I am not watching. I need all these things, Penelope, and more."

"Perhaps you will meet someone else. Someone eligible, who can give you such things," Penelope suggested.

Rebecca shook her head. "It is foolish of me, I know, but there are times when I look at Hugh and think I have always known him. As though no one in the world could matter to me as much as he does. And then he will say or do something which makes me so angry with him I cannot know what to speak."

Even in the darkness Rebecca could feel her sister grin.

"That, at any rate, appears to be true of all men, judging by what I have heard Diana and Annabelle and Barbara tell Mama," Penelope said tartly. "And one reason I wish never to marry. For I would tell a man precisely what I thought, and who would bear with that?"

Rebecca came and sat on the edge of her sister's bed and took her hands in her own. "A man who loved you would," she said.

Penelope snorted and drew her hands free. "Love! An emotion that makes fools out of everyone, so far as I can see. No, I want nothing to do with it. But I can see that for you it is different, Rebecca, and I release you from our pact—if you do find someone to marry whom you can love."

And with those words she reached out to hug her sister and though it was all nonsense, both of them were soon crying. It was, they both knew, the beginning of the end.

Hugh was feeling far less amiable several hours later. It was late, well past midnight, and he was still grim with the discovery of what the ring, or more likely their leader, wished him to do.

Right now he stood outside Philip Caldwell's house, waiting for him to return. Nearby, in the shadows, was at least one witness. Rowland would have to take care of him before he took care of Caldwell, that much was clear. But how? And how to do so without arousing further suspicions against himself?

And then the opportunity came. Caldwell appeared out of the shadows, lurching toward his front door, definitely more than three sheets to the wind. Hugh stepped forward briskly and intercepted him before he could reach his front step. He spoke in low tones that could not be overheard by the man watching.

"This way, sir. Urgent matter for you to attend to. Party. Gaming. High stakes. Just your sort of thing. But you've got to step lively now. Hurry, or you'll be late and miss all the fun."

Caldwell peered, blurry eyed at Hugh. "Do I know you?" he asked, puzzled and trying to hold himself straight.

Hugh linked his arm with Caldwell's and began to move him down the street. "No time to waste," he said. "Come along now."

It would be too much to say that Caldwell was persuaded. Even as bosky as he was, he knew that the man accosting him was dressed as a servant. On the other hand, he spoke precisely like a gentleman. Was the fellow taking part in some sort of wager? And did it matter? He promised Philip fun. He promised gaming with high stakes. Throwing all caution to the wind, Caldwell decided to go with him.

Hugh moved faster and faster, heading vaguely toward the river and side streets where he could lose the man following him. When that proved impossible, Hugh took a deep breath and did what he had to do. He let go of Caldwell's arm, spun him around, and threw a punch into his face. He meant to knock the man out and then pretend to use his knife on him. Unfortunately, he had misgauged his target. Philip Caldwell was in far better shape than anyone could have expected.

Instead of crumpling to the ground, Caldwell fought back. "Want to go a round do you? Strip to advantage, I don't doubt. But so do I. Come on, try it again."

Caldwell wasn't lying. He did know how to fight and gave almost as good as he got. Almost. Finally, as he lay in the street, his chest struggling to take in sufficient air, Hugh held a knife high so that it glittered in the moonlight, then he plunged it toward Caldwell. The man screamed once and then all was silent.

The watcher glided out of the shadows and came up to Hugh. "Done 'im, 'as you? Come on then, let's get 'im into the river."

Hugh tucked away his knife. He swaggered though he didn't move an inch. "Oi'll do it meself. You just go and tell 'un oi've done what oi was asked."

The man hesitated then shrugged. "If'n you don'ts want me 'elp, it's foine wif me."

Hugh waited until he disappeared, then reached down and felt for Caldwell's pulse. It was strong and he sent up a silent prayer of thanks that the man had fainted so conveniently when Hugh showed him the knife. He hadn't even had to knock him out with the handle as he had planned to do.

Still, there wasn't much time. He had to get Caldwell out of sight before the watcher changed his mind and came back. Then he had to get back to Lady Brisbane's household before morning. What a good thing he had run into Farrington this afternoon, after all! He had a fast team of horses and though Sir Parker would not like his enlisting the help of a married man, Rowland knew that with luck Farrington could get Caldwell out of London before anyone was the wiser.

With Caldwell slung over his shoulders, Hugh began to move more swiftly than ever though the dark, damp London streets.

Chapter 12

Hugh avoided everyone the next morning. It wasn't wise to go asking for trouble, and that was what it would be doing to let anyone see his face. He found work to do outside the house and kept his face averted from the other servants. That was where Lady Rebecca found him, sweeping the back path.

He turned, saw her, and smiled before he could stop himself. Then cursed as he saw her own smile fade. The devil take it, she had a way of making him forget himself, forget his training and carefully cultivated caution, forget that he didn't know how to laugh.

Not that either of them was laughing now. She had obviously noticed his blackened eye. And the bruises he could not hide. She gave a tiny cry and reached out to touch his battered face.

"What has happened?" she said indignantly. "Who has done this to you?"

Hugh looked down and sighed. He could scarcely tell her the truth, that he had gotten these bruises murdering a man. Instead, he shrugged.

"No 'un. It were just a foight."

She jumped back, alarmed. "Just a fight? You say that as if you fight all the time."

Hugh shrugged again and made his expression turn surly. "May'aps oi do."

"Fighting is wrong," she said severely.

He tilted his chin up defensively. "Nots if you 'as to do it to survive, m'lydie."

There. That should shock her into dropping the matter. But it didn't.

Rebecca stared at Hugh. Her frown softened. Was that the way of it? That he had to fight, just to survive? It touched her heart and she wanted to reach out and tell him so. But she couldn't. He must learn that most people did not approve of fighting.

"Not while you work in this house," she told him severely. "If one of the other servants is troubling you, you need only tell my aunt."

" 'Tweren't any'un 'ere," Hugh said, not meeting her eyes, which opened wide.

"You were out again last night, weren't you?" she said accusingly. "Oh, Hugh! And yet I know you can change. You must."

Rebecca put a hand on his arm. It trembled, and that gave her hope that she was right. Otherwise, why would he tremble at her touch?

"I know it must be hard for you," she said softly. "You weren't born with the advantages I have had. But I assure you, there are other ways for you to proceed, to live your life. Other than being a thief, I mean. Or fighting on the streets."

Now his arm was trembling even more. He seemed about to tell her something, something important, when Jeffries's voice suddenly called out, interrupting them.

"Hugh! You are wanted above stairs. Now."

Rebecca and Hugh exchanged startled glances. "Oi'd best go in," he said.

She nodded and let him brush past her. Then she followed. There was satisfaction and even, she was dismayed to see, a hint of maliciousness in Jeffries's face as he stood watching Hugh.

Right then and there Rebecca decided to follow Hugh in to see whoever it was who had summoned him. But Miss Tibbles forestalled her. She blocked the way on the stairs and told Rebecca, "Come along. You are behind in your lessons and that I will not allow, even if you are a young lady being brought out this Season."

Rebecca would have argued except there was something in Miss Tibbles's expression that stopped her. She had a strong notion that her governess knew what was going on. If so, perhaps she would tell her. She was right.

In the schoolroom, Miss Tibbles closed the door and turned to Rebecca. And yet it took her some moments before she could speak. Penelope watched, with wide, curious eyes from near the window. Finally, when Rebecca thought she could stand it no longer, the governess began to speak.

"Your father and aunt are going to dismiss Hugh. He has evidently been fighting, and that is one thing they will not allow in this house. You are not to interfere. It would only," Miss Tibbles said, her voice catching, "make matters worse for him."

She paused and tried visibly to collect herself. After a moment, she pressed on. "Do not worry for Hugh. They mean to send him away with some money in his pocket and your aunt has agreed to write him a recommendation. For a masculine household, of course, where perhaps they would take a lighter view of such things. Oh, my dear, I know this is distressing you, but you must believe he will be all right. And you have done your best for him, truly you have!"

Rebecca whirled toward the door. Behind her she heard Miss Tibbles saying something more, but she paid no attention. Instead, she fairly flew down the stairs, only to discover he was already gone. Nothing she said could persuade her parents or her aunt to tell her where. If they even knew and, in honesty, she could not think they did.

Slowly she dragged herself back upstairs where Miss Tibbles and Penelope were waiting. Both tried to coax her into better humor. It was scarcely surprising, however, that they could not succeed.

Out in the street, Hugh pondered his next move. Clearly his cover here was gone. He could not blame the family. The only wonder was that they had kept him on this long.

The thing that hurt the most was Lady Rebecca. He wished he had been able to say good-bye to her, but perhaps it was best he could not. She was a distraction. Worse, she made him begin to feel things he had not felt in years—if he ever had felt them before. She made him begin to believe in things like caring and kindness, that someone might feel those things for him.

And that was dangerous. No, better that he left without seeing her. Better that he get on with what he was supposed to do. But how? How to get closer to the inner ring?

Rowland had a shrewd notion that once Halifax learned he had been dismissed for having a bruised face, it would cause the man to consider him clumsy and all but value-less—unless he could do something to prove otherwise.

There was Sir Parker's jewelry, of course, but that trap was not quite ready to be sprung. No, he needed something that would make him look capable, dangerous, and useful. Hugh thought he knew how to do it. But later. After dark. For now, he would go and speak to Sir Parker and discover if he knew when the group was next expected to meet.

For the sake of anyone watching, Hugh turned and raised a fist toward Lady Brisbane's townhouse. He shook it and shouted several curses. Then, as though he were deep in plans, he headed off down the street.

Rebecca could not bear it. She knew there was some fatal flaw in her character that she could care so deeply about a streetsweep. Still, her oldest sister, Diana, had once loved a groom and when she could bear it no longer, Rebecca sent her maid for her cloak and to arrange for a carriage. She told Miss Tibbles, "I am going to see Diana!"

Miss Tibbles was a very wise woman. She made no effort to stop her, making sure only that Rebecca's maid would accompany her. And Penelope.

It was early, far too early for ordinary callers, and Rebecca knew she would find Diana alone. She might be the Duchess of Berenford, but Rebecca knew she would either be with her daughter or just coming in from a ride in the park or writing letters. And maybe, just maybe, she would have some wisdom for Rebecca.

"Dearest sisters, how are you?" Diana asked, rising to her feet and setting aside her half-finished letter when Rebecca and Penelope were shown in. "Let me see. Ah, Mama is still dressing both of you in pale colors, but at least they become you better than they ever became me. Certainly I have heard that you have won over half the male hearts in London already."

Penelope merely scowled. Rebecca laughed, but half-heartedly. Nor could she summon the energy to truly envy Diana the elegant morning gown of deep green crape that she wore. Both circumstances alarmed Diana, who peered closely at her sister, exchanged significant looks with Penelope, then drew Rebecca to sit on the sofa beside her.

"Tell me what has occurred to overset you," Diana said with a frown, "and there is no use pretending otherwise, for I can see it in your face."

"Diana, how did you feel when you thought you had a *tendre* for a groom?" Rebecca asked.

Her eldest sister colored deeply and looked away, then back again. "The streetsweep?" she asked.

It was Rebecca's turn to flush. "How did you know?"

"Half of London has mentioned the kind heart of the Westcott girl who rescued a streetsweep who had rescued her. So I would know even if Aunt Ariana had not dropped hints in my ear when I met her in the park." Diana paused and looked at her other sister. "Mind you, she is far more concerned about you, Penelope. She swears you will end a spinster!"

The Duchess of Berenford paused, then said, hesitantly, to Rebecca, "Do you really have a *tendre* for him? This streetsweep?"

Miserably Rebecca nodded. "I have tried not to feel this way, but it is not of the slightest use. And now Papa and Aunt Ariana, and Mama too, I suppose, have banished him from the house. Merely because he got into a fight and has bruises all over his face."

Diana started to laugh and then muffled the sound as quickly as she could. "I beg your pardon, my dear, but you must admit, someone with bruises all over his face would be a trifle disconcerting to stare at all day long. How did it happen?"

Rebecca looked away. "He wouldn't say," she said stiffly.

For a long moment her sister was silent, then she leaned forward and put a hand over Rebecca's. "I am sorry. I can see that you do care deeply about this streetsweep of yours. And I wish that there could be as happy an ending for you as there was for me. Only I do not see how."

"Nor do I," Rebecca agreed, a stricken expression upon her face. "I know it is foolish beyond permission. I know that I must look to one of my own for a husband. And I will, for it is my duty to do so. But Diana, how on earth shall I bear to have a husband touch me if I do not feel for him what I do for Hugh?"

"Are you so certain you will not?" Diana asked hesitantly.

She nodded, miserably.

"What do you wish me to say?" Diana persisted, bewildered.

Rebecca smiled wryly. "Just that you do not think the worse of me for having such a foolish heart."

"Oh, Rebecca! As if I could, when my own has been so foolish in its own way!" Diana exclaimed, leaning forward to embrace her sister.

There then ensued a good cry between the two that made them both feel much better. Penelope watched silently, wishing she could help Rebecca.

And when they left to return home, summoning their maid from the kitchen where the woman had been enjoying a comfortable coze of her own with the servants there, Rebecca was a trifle more at ease with herself. Penelope still looked as grim as ever.

No problems had been solved, but at least one person in London truly understood how Rebecca felt, and had once felt the same. Anxious looks from her parents and her aunt and Miss Tibbles were far easier to endure when she knew that at least one person did not judge her for where she had placed her heart. Other than Penelope, of course, who would have defended Rebecca no matter what she did.

Still, it was not an easy evening for Rebecca. The theater could not hold her attention. The compliments of the young gentlemen who crowded into their box during intermission seemed absurd. And yet Rebecca pretended to laugh and flirt, discreetly of course, as she was expected to do. Not for anything would she worry her parents any further. Only Penelope knew what it cost her and she was no happier, wishing as she did that all the gentlemen could be banned from their box forever.

And when they returned home, Rebecca prepared for bed and resolutely steeled herself not to watch from the window tonight. Tonight she would begin a lifetime of trying to forget she had ever known a vagabond and erstwhile thief named Hugh.

That was why she never even noticed when he crept into

the backyard and entered through a ground floor window. And she was fast asleep when he left the note on her pillow and the cat's box on the floor beside her bed.

He wished he could be there to see the kittens born.

Chapter 13

"I would not have thought it of the man!" Lady Westcott cried, dabbing at her eyes as she stared at the note she held. "We were kind to him and this is how he repays us!"

"Deuced strange he left a note," Lord Westcott said with a frown.

"He didn't wish anyone else to be blamed for what he had done," Rebecca said, from her seat by the window.

Lord Westcott looked at his daughter reprovingly even as Lady Brisbane said, "This is what comes of hiring someone entirely without references. I shall certainly never do so again."

"We shall repay you, of course, for the missing silver," the earl said heavily. "It is, after all, our fault he was taken on in the first place."

"Men are never to be trusted," Penelope sniffed from her corner. She was careful, however, not to say it very loudly. Not when her sister was in such distress.

As for Rebecca, she sat by the window, motionless, a hollow sensation at the pit of her stomach. She should have tried harder! If she had stayed closer to him, provided him with greater incentives, perhaps then he would have been able to resist temptation.

It was all her fault. She should never have placed him in the way of temptation in the first place. Perhaps he would have been better off if she had left him on the street. Then he would not have been surrounded by silver or Mama's and Aunt Ariana's jewels. As for the loss of her own pearl necklace, she did not give a fig for that.

And yet, he could not wholly be beyond redemption for he had left a birthing box for the cat. He must have built it with his own hands and already the cat was safely installed in it. There was room for as many kittens as she might have, and sides high enough to keep them in until they could fend for themselves. And when she had gone outside with that, Rebecca had found the bird already settled in a new home he had built for it as well. Would a true villain have done all of that? And yet, if he was not a villain, why had he stolen their things?

With a sigh, ignoring the tempest behind her, Rebecca leaned her forehead against the window, Why, oh, why had she made such a thorough muddle of things? Nor did it help when Lord Halifax was announced.

"We cannot see company now!" Lady Westcott cried.

But it was too late. Halifax was already being shown into the room and Rebecca hastily brushed the tears away from her eyes. She even managed a tremulous smile as she turned to greet him. She would not be the one to betray that a tragedy had occurred.

But he already knew. The moment the door closed behind Lord Halifax he bowed to the ladies and said, "You have my deepest sympathies."

"Then you know?" Lady Westcott exclaimed.

"How do you know?" was her sister's shrewder question.

Halifax turned his hand one way and then the other. "How does one ever learn of such things?" he countered. "I cannot recall who told me of it."

"The servants must have been gossiping again," Lady Brisbane said angrily.

"Perhaps, but that is not important. I came to offer you my condolences," Halifax said. "Particularly you, Lady Rebecca."

Suddenly Rebecca found she hated the man. She would not give him the satisfaction of being able to pity her. She straightened her shoulders, tossed back her head, and managed a little laugh.

"I? Why should you feel sorry for me, Lord Halifax? I have only lost a pearl necklace. My mother and aunt have lost far worse."

He looked at his cane, then at her. There was a thin smile upon his face as he said, "Perhaps I was mistaken, but I thought you had a kindness for the fellow."

Lady Westcott looked stricken, but Rebecca needed no such warning. There was already a martial gleam in her eyes as she replied lightly, "How absurd! I told you the other day that I have far more important matters on my mind than one servant more or less in the household."

His brows rose in surprise. "Such as?"

"Why, the next ball we attend, of course," Rebecca laughed.

He accepted her answer as though he believed she felt as carefree as that. Inside, Rebecca thrust down all the pain and forced herself to manage a careless conversation until Halifax finally, to her relief, took his leave. It was, after all, only a taste of things to come and she had best learn to deal with it now. But if she ever, Rebecca thought, did see Hugh again, she was going to thoroughly wring his neck for placing her in such an awkward situation!

Fortunately for Rebecca, her mother and her aunt guessed none of her thoughts. They even expressed pleasure at the sensibleness of her outlook, once Halifax was gone. Only Penelope looked unconvinced and looked at her sister with both sympathy and dismay.

Rebecca listened as her mother and aunt made plans for an expedition to replace at least some of the pieces that were gone. It seemed the Bow Street Runner her father had summoned first thing that morning had told them he doubted the jewelry would ever be found.

When told to come along, Rebecca tried to decline. She had, she said, to practice the pianoforte. Any other day, it was an answer that would have been acceptable, if bewildering, to her poor mother, but today it was not. Reluctantly, she rose to her feet and prepared to go with them to Rundell and Bridge, the jewelers.

Hugh moved steadily toward his goal. The jewelry and silver from Lady Brisbane's household were safely stashed away. For now. He hated having had to steal their valuables, but at least it should persuade Halifax his interest had been in what profit he could find.

He felt a pang of regret go through him as he considered what Lady Rebecca must be feeling. Betrayal would be the least of it. Somehow he knew she would be worried about him, he thought with a wry smile.

But he did not dare dwell on that, he told himself sternly. He had work to do and he could not afford to let his attention lapse. Matters were moving faster than he, than anyone, had expected.

Hugh paused, looked around, then began to move silently through the crowds again. He spotted his quarry, Sir Parker, some distance ahead of him. As arranged, the man was just now emerging from Rundell and Bridge, the jewelers, and was strolling as though he had not a care in the world.

Hugh was also well aware of the three men in the crowd who were watching *him* as well as Sir Parker. No doubt they had been entrusted with the job of lifting the jewelry piece from Sir Parker's pocket. But Hugh intended to do it for them. They eyed him nervously, as though wondering what he was doing there, wondering if they should distrust him.

Well, that was all right. He wouldn't trust himself either, in their shoes. Hugh smiled to himself as he closed the gap with Sir Parker. The old gentleman was doing a perfect imitation of a bumbling fool oblivious to his surroundings. But Hugh knew that Sir Parker could no doubt have described everyone and everything near him and that he was exquisitely alert.

The plan was that Sir Parker was to allow Hugh to steal the jewelry piece and then, when he was somewhat farther down the street, "discover" the theft and raise a fuss that would divert attention while Hugh disappeared. That way he would have time to hide the piece before the ring of thieves could take it from him.

It would be nip and tuck, for Hugh had no illusions about the skill of the men he was working with. Their leader employed only the best. But he would manage it. Too much depended on it for him to fail at this point.

Ah, now he was right behind Sir Parker. A quick dip of his hand and there it was. Now back away, carefully. The others were still giving him room.

Suddenly a shout went up. "Thief! A thief has taken my necklace!"

Sir Parker's shrill voice drew everyone's attention and soon all eyes were on him. Hugh slipped around a corner and began to run. Now he slowed. Another corner and again he ran. Twisting, turning through the streets of London. Until he was certain he was running alone.

He would be at the rendezvous tonight. But on his terms, not theirs. And he would tell them he would turn the jewelry and his loot from the Westcott household only over to the man he had met before.

Hugh felt a grim sense of satisfaction that all had gone so well. It is not certain he would have felt nearly so pleased had he known that the entire escapade had been witnessed by the Westcott family and Lady Brisbane as they stood, mouths agape, on the sidewalk outside Rundell and Bridge, too frozen in shock to even cry out a warning. But had he known, it still would not have changed a thing.

It did, however, change Rebecca's feelings greatly. She knew the sight of him as well as she knew her own reflection in the looking glass. And it was Hugh, slipping his fingers into that man's pockets, and then turning down an alleyway the moment the shouting began.

She wanted very much to run after him, to tell him to please come back and return the jewels and silver to her parents and aunt and whatever it was he had stolen from the man. She wanted to promise she really, really would try harder to help him resist temptation.

But Rebecca did none of those things. To do so would have put her beyond the pale where perhaps, she thought with a burst of self-pity, she already belonged. Instead, she dutifully followed her father and mother and aunt into the shop of Rundell and Bridge. There, when commanded to do so, she and Penelope described their matching pearl necklaces in soft voices that scarcely trembled at all.

"I think we can match that," the jeweler said kindly. "And some of the other pieces as well. Though it may take a little time. Meanwhile, I shall put out word that your jewelry was taken. If the fellow attempts to sell some of it, particularly any of the more unusual pieces, to one of my fellow jewelers, perhaps it can be retrieved at a reasonable cost."

"Reasonable cost!" Lady Westcott exclaimed. "But why should we have to pay a penny? It belonged to us."

The jeweler coughed discreetly. "Well, yes, but as to that, you are prepared to pay me to replace the pieces. Surely, if it can be done, it makes sense to pay a smaller price and retrieve the originals, if we can."

"It does make sense," Lady Brisbane agreed.

"Aye, though it goes against the grain with me, I have to agree as well," Lord Westcott said grudgingly. He eyed the jeweler for a moment and then added, "You're an honest man, sir. You might have done just as you've said and never told us, but presented the pieces to us as new and pocketed the difference. Stap me, but I'll trust you on this and here's my hand on the matter."

The jeweler took it, again assured them he would do his best, and bowed the entire party out of the shop. Rebecca looked around eagerly, but of course there was no sign of Hugh. How could there be? He must be long gone by now. The man who had been robbed, however, was still there and loudly proclaiming the wrong that had been done against him.

"Perhaps I should put a word in his ear as to who it might have been," Lord Westcott said, hesitating on the sidewalk.

"No, Papa!" Rebecca cried. When he gaped at her she went on quickly, lowering her voice so they would not be overheard, "Do you wish him to know we harbored a criminal? How would you explain knowing his name? Seeing him and not crying out a warning?"

"Dearest, no," Lady Westcott entreated her husband.

"She has a point," Lady Brisbane put in.

Westcott looked once more in the direction of the man, and then shrugged. "Very well. After all, what good would it do him anyway? It's not as if we could give him the man's direction. Come along now. We've had enough excitement for one day."

"More than enough," Lady Westcott agreed emphatically.

Rebecca came. And if her eyes kept darting from side to side hoping and at the same time fearing she might see Hugh, well, who was to know what she was thinking? Except perhaps Penelope, of course.

The night was overcast and very dark. It bothered neither Hugh nor the men standing before him.

" 'E wants the sparklers," one of the men told Hugh.

Hugh shifted his weight, preparing himself should the others decide to attack. "Oi'll gives 'em only to the guv'nor meself," he said belligerently.

"Oh? And if we decides to takes 'em from you?" someone else demanded.

"Oi don'ts 'aves 'em wif me," Hugh said, shoving out his jaw. "And won'ts until after oi've seen 'im."

Someone took a step toward Hugh. But the other had his orders. "Come wif me," he said.

The twists and turns were different from the ones he had been taken on before. The final result, however, was very much the same—a darkened room with a candle that lit only Hugh's face.

"Well?" the voice said out of the darkness.

Hugh was more certain than ever that it was Halifax. He crossed his arms, and stood cockily as he said, "Oi've got it. Wots it worf to you?"

"You know the agreement," the voice replied, anger kept tightly in check. "You give me what I tell you to give me and I don't have you killed."

"Oi wants more'n that," Hugh countered. "Oi wants to 'ave a say in wot we does."

Hesitation, as though Halifax were considering the matter. "Why?" he demanded at last.

"Oi wants a say," Hugh repeated stubbornly.

Another long silence and then, to the evident surprise of the man who had brought Hugh here, Halifax agreed. "Very well. Bring the piece tomorrow night and I will introduce you to those of us who make the decisions. We will hear what you have to say. But," Halifax's voice dropped low and dangerous, "if you try to betray us or we find you not worth listening to, you will not live to see the following morning."

"Roight enough, guv'nor," Hugh said cheerfully, as if he were not in the least daunted.

And then he was following the other man out a door other than the one they had entered. This time there were no drains, but it was small consolation. Clearly, this was as temporary a location as the last one had been. Tomorrow, he hoped, he would get to see the real center of where they belonged.

Chapter 14

Candles flickered and Hugh was acutely aware of the circle of men and the hoods that covered their faces. The room had sufficient illumination that he could see the heavy chairs they each sat upon and the hoods that covered their heads. It was yet another location, one he had not seen before, and he began to wonder if they ever met in one place twice.

The paste jewelry he had taken from Sir Parker was in his pocket and the packet of jewels and silver he had taken from the Westcotts was on the table before him. Hugh slowly drew Sir Parker's bait out of his pocket and noted grimly the way all eyes lit up at the sight of what he held. The jewels seemed to shimmer in the candlelight.

"Well done," a familiar voice said. "Hand it over now and you'll be well rewarded."

Hugh did so, his senses acutely alert for treachery. But Halifax was in an amiable mood.

"Gentlemen," Halifax said, "regard this man carefully. He is one of the most promising additions to our group yet. Who wishes to set him the next task?"

There was a clamor of voices and Halifax allowed it to go on for several moments. Then he held up a hand and silence instantly fell over the group.

"I heard Lady Pickworth's name mentioned. Excellent suggestion. There is word that she has just received a present of rubies of incomparable quality. Can anyone tell me when she will be likely to leave them unguarded?"

Again the voices clamored. This time there could be no agreement, except that it would be impossible to name a time and place and date.

"She is so suspicious she has men prowl about the grounds at night."

"And dogs. Don't forget the dogs," another added.

"Very large dogs," said a third.

Finally, their leader grew weary of the noise. He held up a hand and said, humor in his voice as he addressed Rowland, "You have proven your worth as a pickpocket and as a thief, but it would seem Lady Pickworth's rubies are a far more daunting task. Do you wish to risk it?"

"Yes."

"How?" someone asked. "We've told you she is uncannily suspicious."

Hugh hesitated. Where, he wondered, were Sir Parker's men? He had promised to let one of them give the signal when he judged it the right moment to capture this crowd.

Meanwhile, these men were waiting for his answer. Rowland must spin it out and keep them captivated, at least for now. He tilted his head to one side and pretended to swagger

"Woi, oi thinks it roight easy. One, or p'rhaps several, of you will wroite me letters of recommendation. Oi'll arrange to be 'oired on as a member of her 'ouse'old, oi will," Hugh said coolly.

"Preposterous!" someone exclaimed.

"Who would hire you?"

"You don't sound like a servant!"

Hugh allowed himself to change. Subtly he shifted, stood more erect, and in a voice closer to that of a proper servant than a cockney vagabond he said, "I have done so before, you know."

There was absolute, shocked silence as each man considered whether all of his own servants were what they seemed to be. And whether they could be trusted. Only their leader was amused.

"Indeed you have," Halifax said. "And quite successfully, by the looks of what you have brought us tonight. But that is a part which can only be played so often before you are seen and recognized," he pointed out.

Hugh grinned and tilted his head cockily. "If oi don'ts wants to be recognized, oi warrants you oi won'ts be. Do you be fancying me wif me yeller 'air, or wif black or maybe even red?"

There was a gasp, but also a little laughter at this sudden change back in accent. Only Halifax studied Hugh in silence, as though trying to understand him. Hugh shifted nervously, both because Halifax would expect it and because he truly was getting nervous. Where the devil were Sir Parker's men?

"Very well. It is settled," Halifax said abruptly. "You will shortly have your letters of recommendation. And then you will arrange to be hired on at the Pickworth household—if you can. You will fetch the rubies and the moment you have them, send word to me. We will reconvene then," Halifax announced, rising to his feet.

Some of the others started to rise as well, but one man stayed seated. From beneath his robe came a pistol and he pointed it at each of the others in turn as he said, "No one is going anywhere."

He looked at Rowland and said, "I think we have both heard enough. You may summon help."

Hugh pulled out a whistle and blew it. Instantly, there was a pounding on the steps coming from above and men burst into the room. It was the Bow Street Runners, led by Sir Parker's men.

There was confusion and some fighting, but eventually all save the man with the pistol and Hugh were being led away. The man removed the hood from his face and grinned. He held out his hand and Hugh shook it.

"I was very glad to see that pistol," Hugh said.

"And I to hear you blow the whistle," the other countered. "Sir Parker has interesting conceits. He said you could be

counted on to use it in time but, well, it was a near thing.
Had they reacted a bit quicker, it could have been very bleak
for us."

Hugh nodded and together they followed the others upstairs. Next door a ball was in full sway. Across the street,
Sir Parker was waiting in a carriage, one among many apparently there for the ball.

Hugh and his new friend both climbed up inside. As the
coach clattered along to Mayfair, the two men gave Sir
Parker their reports.

When they were done, Sir Parker nodded. "Excellent. Between the two of you, your testimony will be invaluable in
convicting Halifax. And the others."

He paused and looked at Hugh thoughtfully, then said,
"Although perhaps we'd best get Caldwell back to London
as well. Not only does he belong with the rest, but he may,
knowing Halifax wished him dead, be willing to testify
against the man."

Hugh nodded. "I shall have to go and see Farrington. He
arranged for Caldwell to be spirited out of London for me
and he will need to have him fetched back."

Sir Parker frowned. "I still cannot like using someone who
is not one of us, and someone who is married, at that!"

Hugh grinned. "There wasn't much time. I was told to kill
Caldwell and get rid of his body at once. I had no place to
hide him. As for Farrington, he is a good man and one to be
trusted completely. He's helped me before."

"In the Peninsula?"

Hugh nodded. Sir Parker grunted. "Very well, we'll set
you down at Farrington's household. When you've done
with him, come back to my townhouse. There are still some
loose ends to be wrapped up before Hugh the street thief dis-
appears and Hugh Rowland, gentleman, reappears."

It was very strange, Rebecca thought, looking around the
ballroom. So many gentlemen were missing. They had

drifted away, one by one, and none had yet returned. Including a few to whom she had promised dances. She was not the only one who seemed to notice. As the hour grew later, a number of ladies began to look around, restlessly.

With a frown, Rebecca realized that if she thought back, she could recall that most of these ladies had been accompanied by husbands or brothers or other gentlemen. Gentlemen who were no longer anywhere to be seen. Even Mama seemed to sense that something was wrong. She signaled to Rebecca to come to her once the current song was over.

"Perhaps, dearest, we ought to go," Lady Westcott said hesitantly.

"Yes, please let us do so!" Penelope agreed fervently.

They all looked to Lady Brisbane, who said slowly, "Perhaps we should. A cloud seems to have settled over this room. I wonder why."

But there could be no answer to this. As they called for their carriage, they discovered many others were doing the same. Even the musicians in the ballroom behind them were faltering, and the music came to a halt.

Outside, it was a bright, clear night and Rebecca wondered where Hugh was right now. And what he was doing.

How could she have been so wrong about the man? How could she have given her heart to someone who would trounce it so thoroughly?

And yet she could not help remembering how he had looked at her, how he had kissed her. Surely there had been some feeling for her there?

To be sure, it would have been foolish for either of them to believe it was possible to marry, but surely he had cared enough to wish not to hurt her as he had?

Across town, Lady Tarren waited, either for Lord Halifax to show, or for a note to come explaining why he could not. She devoutly hoped it was the latter. She was weary of pandering to his tastes and she wanted it all over and done with. But that was something that was out of her hands. She could only hope and wait.

And as she waited, Lady Tarren spared more than a thought for the unlikely man who had caught her heart. She didn't want to want him, for it was hopeless, she knew. And yet, nothing her mind said had the faintest impact upon her heart.

There were those who would say she had no heart. But Lady Tarren knew different. It was a pity she could never say so to *him*. But when she had undertaken this role, she had also undertaken a vow to protect the knowledge of their acquaintance. She had not known she would come to love him.

He had not looked at her with longing then, and she somehow did not think he would look at her with longing now. But she could hope. Wait and hope. Sometimes it seemed as if she spent her entire life doing both.

She was still waiting when he came near dawn. Some impulse had made her put off the seductive clothing Lord Halifax would expect her to be wearing. Instead, she had dressed in a morning gown any lady in London could have worn. Any respectable lady.

For this moment, she could pretend she had never been ruined, never faced such gossip that it drove her to wilder and wilder excess, until she was entirely cast out of the *ton*. Until Sir Parker offered her the chance for redemption, the chance to help her country.

She had even moved to the little sitting room she kept for moments when she wanted to remember what her life once had been. He found her there, drinking tea.

"Sir Parker! It is over then?"

He nodded, his shrewd eyes taking in her gown, her hair done up on the top of her head, the sitting room he had never seen before.

"It is," he agreed. He paused and cleared his throat. "I came to thank you for your help."

Her hand went to her own throat in a gesture she was not conscious of making. "I—You're welcome, sir."

For a long moment, they stared at one another, and then she forced herself to give a little laugh as she said, in a high, artificial voice, "Well, and so do you know what assignment you will give me next?"

He almost took a step toward her, but stopped. Instead, he looked down at the floor. "I, er, haven't considered the matter yet." Then, because he was no coward, he looked up and met her eyes. In a somewhat stronger voice he said, "I was thinking that perhaps we wouldn't need your services anymore."

A stricken look crossed her face, but she swiftly hid it. "Oh. I see. Of course. Thank you for coming to tell me so in person."

He shook his head impatiently. "I am not dismissing you because I think you cannot be of help. I am thinking of you. That this may not be what you wish to do anymore."

She gave a laugh, forced and shrill. "Not wish to do it? But my dear sir, what else will I do with myself?"

He looked at her and it seemed there was a profound sadness in his eyes as he said, "Why, anything you wish. But if I was mistaken . . ."

"Oh, you were, I assure you," she said.

Sir Parker nodded and turned to go. "Very well. Then I shall send word when I know how best we can use you next."

He got as far as the door before he paused again. He turned and looked at her one last time but could think of nothing to say. And so he simply left.

Sir Parker never saw the tears that began, one by one, to tumble down Lady Tarren's cheeks. Nor the hiss of indrawn breath that was her only defense against the urge she felt to run after him and call him back.

But she would not do so. Sir Parker was an honorable man. A respectable gentleman. And it had been far too many years since anyone had called Lady Tarren either honorable or respectable. No, she could not, would not call him back.

Slowly, Lady Tarren rose to her feet and began to unpin her hair. It had been foolish to think she could pretend to be someone she was not.

Even more slowly, she mounted the stairs to her bedroom. Not the one Lord Halifax, or any of the other gentlemen, had seen, but the one where she took refuge on the nights she knew she would be alone.

The bedroom that resembled nothing so much as the one she had slept in before she was married. Before she became the woman everyone knew she now was.

Chapter 15

The Westcotts and Lady Brisbane were sitting around the breakfast table when the package arrived. A very large parcel it was, too. Inside were Lady Brisbane's silver and her jewels and in another parcel was all of the jewelry belonging to Lord Westcott's ladies.

There was also a very simple note. It apologized for whatever distress may have been caused by the temporary borrowing of these items.

"Temporary borrowing indeed!" Lord Westcott exclaimed with a snort. "Thievery, pure and simple, that's what I call it."

"Yes, dear, but he did return the things," Lady Westcott temporized.

"Someone did, at any rate," Lady Brisbane countered dryly. "We have no proof it was the same one who took them."

Now Rebecca, who had been staring at the parcels with something of a dazed look upon her face, said, her eyes shining, "Oh, but it must have been! I am certain it was Hugh who sent these things back."

"Oh, really?" the earl asked. "Then tell me, Rebecca, why did he take them in the first place?"

A frown crossed her face. "Perhaps he could not help himself," she said slowly. "But then, when he had had them for a little while, he realized he could not keep them. Surely that means he is learning to be more honest?"

Another snort was the only answer Lord Westcott cared to give. Lady Westcott and her sister exchanged speaking glances and it was Penelope who said, "Oh, Rebecca, do stop this nonsense! You cannot go on believing you can save that man. Yes, perhaps he returned these things. But it is more likely that it was because the Bow Street Runners, whom Papa set on his trail, were growing too close and he wished to be rid of the evidence, than because of a sudden burst of honesty on his part."

At these words, Rebecca burst into tears and fled from the table. The others shook their heads in silent sympathy.

"I knew no good could come of hiring that man," Lady Westcott said with a sniff.

Upstairs, Rebecca threw herself on her bed and cried. It could not be true, surely, Penelope's cynical words? And if it was, so what? She only hoped Hugh had escaped whatever trap the Bow Street Runners had set for him. And meanwhile, she did not wish to talk to anyone in her family. Not when they showed themselves so unsympathetic to the poor fellow.

The rest of the family might have thought it wise to accede to her wishes in this respect, but not Miss Tibbles. Upon leaving the breakfast table, Penelope ran straight to the governess and told her the tale.

Miss Tibbles immediately went in search of Rebecca.

"Come now," she said briskly, "time for your lessons!"

"I should not have to do lessons," Rebecca replied with a sniff. "I am a young lady already going to balls. It is past time Penelope and I were done with such things. Other girls are."

Miss Tibbles advanced toward her charge, a martial gleam in her eyes. "That's as may be," she said, "but in this household you are not done with your lessons until I say you are, and it is very clear to me that you and your sister can still greatly benefit from being forced to use your minds. Now come along, your sister is waiting!"

Since she knew that Miss Tibbles was quite capable of
enforcing this command with a bucket of cold water or by
grasping her ear, Rebecca went.

And indeed, there was something comforting about having her mind distracted by doing sums and studying the
globe and writing down a treatise on a passage from one of
her Latin books.

Hugh Rowland paused on the steps of Lady Brisbane's
townhouse, as so many young gentlemen had paused there
before him, and tugged at his cravat, just as they had done.

He shouldn't be here. He shouldn't be talking with anyone, except a court of law, about what he had done. Sir
Parker had been none too pleased to give him the letter he
had asked for.

And yet he was here. Rowland couldn't help himself, it
seemed. With a scowl he told himself he was only here to
set matters straight with the Westcott family, because he
owed them the truth. And that was, that could be, the only
reason he was here.

The trouble was, Hugh couldn't make even himself believe such a bouncer. He was here to see Lady Rebecca. To
make certain she was all right. Because he could guess how
his desertion must have seemed to her. And to do that, he
had first to get past her father, which was not likely to
prove an easy task. Before he could lose his courage, he
rapped on the door.

By not one flicker of his eyelids did Jeffries betray that
he recognized the man before him. Instead, he took the note
Rowland handed him and asked him to wait. A few minutes
later he returned, took his hat and gloves, and led him into
the library to see Lord Westcott.

The earl rose to his feet, but his expression was distinctly
hostile. "When Jeffries told me you were here, I could not
believe your infernal impudence. Or that you had the au-
dacity to present yourself as Hugh Rowland, a gentleman.

But I see that he was telling me the truth. Can you give me one reason I should not send for the Bow Street Runners?" Lord Westcott demanded.

Rowland did not smile. Instead, he answered gravely, "I understand your anger. In your place I would feel the same. But I beg you will read the letter I bring you from Lord Farrington. And a similar one from Sir Parker, with whom I believe you are a little acquainted."

Westcott took the proffered notes. He did not ask Rowland to sit and Hugh stood as he waited for the earl to read the notes. Finally, when he was done, the earl looked up at him, a bemused expression upon his face.

"Both my son-in-law and Sir Parker appear to think highly of you. They tell me you have an interesting tale to tell and that I would be well advised to listen to it. For their sakes I shall give you ten minutes."

Hugh briefly told him about the mission he had undertaken and about the arrests the night before. When he was done, he could see that the earl had thawed slightly. Still, he was not entirely won over.

Lord Westcott cleared his throat and his voice was anything but warm as he said sardonically, "That is all very well. Commendable, even, perhaps. But I pray you will tell me why you felt the need to masquerade as a servant in this house. And to steal the silver and jewelry. We have gone through a great deal of distress and discomfort and inconvenience because of it, you know!"

"I do know, and I am very sorry for it. I never meant to intrude upon this household," Hugh said quietly. "But when your daughter was shoved into the street I could not help rescuing her. And then she, in turn, insisted upon rescuing me. Very persistent she was, sir."

The earl shifted uncomfortably in his seat. "Yes, well, Rebecca can be damnably persistent, I will give you that. But why agree to take a post in this house? And why steal our valuables?"

Hugh spread his hands. "It seemed an excellent cover. And since we knew these houses had been targeted, we knew the thieves we wanted to catch would be watching. I needed a way to ingratiate myself with their leader, Lord Halifax, and prove my worth so that I would be allowed to attend a meeting of them all. We needed, you see, to tie all the pieces together in order to unmask them completely."

For several very long moments, the earl was silent. Finally he said, bending a piercing gaze upon the other, "My daughter was very fond of the servant named Hugh."

For the first time since he entered the room, Hugh smiled. "You have a remarkable daughter, my lord. It is a pity that I am not a marrying man."

The earl blinked. He looked as though he were trying to decide whether to be offended. In the end he said, gruffly, "That is very plain speaking."

"I am a very plain man," Hugh replied quietly. "I felt it my duty to come and explain to you what I did, and to speak to Lady Rebecca as well, if you will allow it. But I wish to deceive neither of you as to my intentions."

"If that is indeed how you feel, then you had best speak to my daughter," Lord Westcott said, an edge to his voice, "and tell her she need spare you no more of her thoughts or compassion. I give you fair warning, she will not be pleased. On the other hand, perhaps she will be so angry you deceived her with your disguise, that she will be happy to see the back of you!"

Hugh merely inclined his head.

"Stay here and I shall send Rebecca in to you," Westcott said heavily. "I have no wish to start an uproar with the rest of the household by having them catch a glimpse of you and then having to explain what you have done. They will find out soon enough as it is."

Hugh agreed. It was a small but comfortably furnished room and had he not been so tall, his stride so long, he would never have felt cramped as he paced waiting for Lady Rebecca. He had no doubt she would be angry.

He also hoped that she would be relieved to discover that her instincts had been more true than anything her head tried to tell her. Hugh kept remembering how she had berated herself for caring about a streetsweep and he would not, could not, leave before he relieved that fear, at least.

But court her he would not. Not with the memory of Felicity so clearly before him. Surely, now that he was no longer the hapless Hugh in need of her help, Lady Rebecca would have no further interest in him?

A pity he could not persuade himself to believe that bouncer either.

Rebecca wasn't smiling. Papa had said there was someone in the library she would wish to see. But she could not conceive who he would wish her to meet in there, his private sanctum in her aunt's house. It was all very mysterious and most unusual. She could only hope it was not an importunate suitor wishing to make her an offer.

Still, she was in general a dutiful daughter and Rebecca took time only to smooth down her skirts before she quietly opened the door to the library.

A gentleman stood by the window, his back to the door, and he did not turn when she entered. How curious!

"Sir?" she said, an inquiring note to her voice.

He turned, then, and her mouth gaped open. Her first instinct was to tell him to hide. Her second to scold him. Her third to doubt the evidence of her eyes.

"Hugh?" she gasped in disbelief.

He nodded.

Rebecca stared at him. He looked impossibly handsome, dressed as he was to the nines. A neatly tied cravat, a wellfitted jacket, his hair trimmed, all these complemented the laughing blue eyes she had already fallen in love with. But what did they have to do with the man she knew as a vagabond and a thief?

He rubbed the side of his nose, ruefully, and suddenly he was the same Hugh as before. Rebecca wanted to go to him, to throw herself into his arms and clasp him tight. Instead, some instinct made her stand near the door, careful to close it against interested ears that might try to overhear their conversation. Then she clasped her hands together to keep from reaching out toward him.

"What are you doing here?" she asked, bewildered. "And why hasn't Papa called the Bow Street Runners? I know you returned the jewelry you took, and the silver, but Mama and Papa and Aunt Ariana are still most distressed!"

Was he actually nervous? He seemed so, his color was high and his hand gripped the back of a chair so tightly his knuckles were white. Good. He deserved to feel at least some of the discomfort that had been her constant companion since he disappeared with their possessions.

"I've spoken to your father and explained everything," he said stiffly. "I assure you, he understands that I only did what I had to do."

"I see. He understands why you had to steal our things?"

"Yes."

"And he understands how a streetsweeping vagabond has become a gentleman overnight?"

"Well, I always was a gentleman," Hugh told her apologetically. "There are, you see, a few things I forgot to tell you."

"Forgot?"

"Well, things I could not tell you," he amended.

She would not shout, she would not scream, she would not faint or have a fit, she told herself sternly. She would wait calmly until he explained.

Hugh told her much the same story he had told her father. And when he was done, it was his turn to wait. Rebecca stared at him, then frowned, then paced over to the window where she stared down at the garden in back of the house. At last she turned and faced him.

"So you never really needed me? My attempts to help you must have seemed such folly!"

His own face mirrored her distress and he took a step toward her. "I never thought you foolish," he said, shaken.

She took a very deep breath. "No? Then why didn't you trust me? Why didn't you tell me the truth about yourself? Why didn't you tell me what you were doing? I would have kept your secret, and you must have known it."

He recoiled, visibly taken aback. "You're a lady," he said. "You ought to be protected from such things. I may make a poor gentleman, but I know that much."

Did he? She wondered who had taught him that lesson. And how. But his other words caught her attention as well. "What do you mean, you think yourself a very poor gentleman?" she asked puzzled. "Do you mean you have not very much money?"

He flushed. "On the contrary, I am quite wealthy," he countered. "Almost indecently so."

"Then whatever did you mean?"

He sighed, clearly not wanting to tell her. He half turned away and his voice was curt as he said, "I am clumsy, ill-spoken, with no ready words to please a lady. I can dance but not gracefully. I do not dress in the latest style, except when I absolutely must. In short, I am no fit companion for a lady."

"I see."

And she did. Someone had hurt Hugh deeply, had lied to him, made him feel not half the man he so very clearly was. Rebecca did not consider herself a violent person, but had it been possible, she would have taken great delight in milling down whoever had done so.

But Hugh misunderstood her silence. Still turned half away, he said, "So you see, you are fortunate I am not a marrying man."

"Oh, undoubtedly," Rebecca said tartly.

That startled him into looking at her. She grinned, unabashedly. "You goose!" she told him fondly. "As if I could believe such farradiddles! If you were truly a clumsy, graceless man, you would never have made a successful thief, sir. As for the rest, I have no patience with it. Nor should you."

Hope dawned on his face, quickly suppressed. He grimaced and said, stiffly, "You are very kind and still, no doubt, trying to rescue me. But it will not do. I am not the proper man for you, and the sooner we both acknowledge it, the better."

Rebecca stared at Hugh. He was retreating into himself. Setting a wall between them. He was like a wild creature, ready to flee, and the more she reached out, the faster he would turn tail and run. So she set herself to coax his trust. Just as she had coaxed the trust of so many wild creatures before.

"How very sensible," she agreed lightly. "And absolutely true."

He gaped at her, his face almost comical in its expression of dismay. Rebecca kept her face solemn, fighting the impulse to laugh. But then, she didn't really feel like laughing. She felt like crying for the man he had once been and wishing she had been there to protect him.

But they were both here now. And she had to consider the possibility that she was wrong. That Hugh had never been hurt, but simply didn't want her. So she waited.

He struggled to find his voice. Finally he said, with some constraint, "You are young and wealthy and very beautiful. You will certainly find a husband in short order. I wish you every happiness when you do."

She shook her head. "I am not certain I wish for one."

"All women do," he persisted.

Rebecca regarded him steadily. There were many things she could have said. In the end she opted for the truth.

What matter that her mother or aunt or governess would be appalled. There was a time for propriety and a time when honesty mattered more. The stakes were too high for her to hide behind propriety or even pride.

"The only husband I am likely to wish for, it seems is not likely to wish for me."

It was an impasse. He stared at her, both longing and wariness in his deep blue eyes. It was himself he was fighting, not her. For a moment, she dared to think she had won.

And then he turned to go. Rebecca stood still, her back very straight, her chin tilted high. She had done her best. If, after all her eloquence, the baring of her soul, he did not want her, she could only let him go.

She could not resist saying, however, to his departing back, "The cat has had her kittens."

He paused. Over his shoulder he said, "How are they?"

"All well. Would you like one?"

He hesitated, then shook his head. "I would have no use nor way to care for it," he said.

And then he was gone.

Chapter 16

If Rebecca could have avoided going to the ball that evening, she would have done so. She tried to get out of it, but no one would listen. It wasn't that she expected to see Hugh there, it was more that she didn't want to see anyone else. It was as if she were afraid they would be able to see on her face all that she felt.

"I don't wish to go," she said. "I have the headache. I think I shall stay home."

"If Rebecca stays home, then I shall stay home," Penelope promptly vowed. "I never wanted to go anyway, and only agreed to go for her sake."

Lady Westcott looked helplessly from one girl to the other, and Lord Westcott felt no better. It was left to Lady Brisbane and Miss Tibbles to handle the matter.

"You will go," Lady Brisbane said, "for my sake. My old friend Cordelia would never forgive me if I did not bring the two of you."

"You will go in your shifts, if need be," Miss Tibbles added, arms crossed and ready for battle, "or I shall dress you as I see fit."

Then, because Miss Tibbles always knew everything that was going on, she said, softly so that only Rebecca could hear, "What? Have you turned coward? Suppose Mr. Rowland is there? Do you mean to give up on him so easily?"

That did it. Rebecca felt herself stiffen. She and Penelope looked at one another. Then slowly, with as much dignity as she could muster, Rebecca climbed the stairs to their room. Penelope followed and they both dressed far more quickly and with less complaint than their maid had ever known them to do before. She, at least, was very pleased.

Soon they stood at the head of the stairs, two lovely young ladies in matching white gowns. They came down slowly, but they did come, and moments later were bundled into the carriage with Lady Westcott and Lady Brisbane. Grumbling, Lord Westcott reluctantly followed.

The line of carriages at Lady Merriweather's house gave gratifying testimony to how well liked she was and how eager everyone was to attend her balls. Inside, they stood in line to greet their hostess, who was a plump, happy creature who was giving the ball to announce the betrothal of her niece.

Lady Brisbane and Lady Merriweather embraced in the glow of the candlelight and then Lady Merriweather tapped Lady Brisbane with her fan.

"Did you hear? Lord Halifax and several other young gentlemen have been arrested! For being part of a ring of thieves!"

Lady Westcott went very pale. Lord Westcott looked everywhere but at his hostess. Lady Brisbane managed to mumble, "How very extraordinary!"

Lady Merriweather nodded, then turned to greet her next guests. The Westcott party, however, soon discovered that the arrests were the main source of gossip tonight. And many of the people present remembered Lord Halifax's interest in Rebecca. They also mistook her disjointed responses to be concern for him. She did not know how to answer, for obviously the truth would not serve.

And then she saw Hugh. He looked so handsome, just as he had this morning, in the library. Seeing him now, all her old fears swept back. Her original fear that he would end in jail, facing the hangman's rope. Then her fear that she would lose him to a past he could not escape. That she would lose her heart to a man she could never have.

And she had. He didn't want her. Or so he had said this morning. But Rebecca remembered how he had looked at her when she thought he was a mere vagabond. She remembered the taste of his lips on her own. And she remembered how he had turned away to keep from embracing her again.

He might say he didn't want her. He might think he didn't need her. But he was wrong. Hugh Rowland, gentleman, needed her as much as Hugh the vagabond ever had. Perhaps even more. And she would no more turn her back on him now than she had been able to turn her back on him then.

With dismay she saw that wherever he walked, people drew aside. Someone would start to speak to him and someone else would pull that person away. It only took a short time for the gossip to reach Rebecca's ears, though she guessed what it must be.

"He is the cause of Lord Halifax's arrest!"

"Yes, I heard he entrapped him. Tricked him perhaps."

"He's the one who ought to be in jail."

"Now, now, I heard that Halifax was guilty, all right and tight. Fellow was only doing his job."

"Doing his job? Betraying one of his own? I scarcely think so! If he thought Halifax up to no good he should have spoken to the man, given him a chance to leave the country, rather than encourage a scandal like this!"

"Yes, and what about all the other young men, innocents drawn into things for amusement. They scarcely deserve to be sent to prison."

"Or hung!"

"Rowland ought to have minded his own business! Why, I heard he masqueraded as a thief himself! Why isn't he in jail?"

Rebecca burned with anger. She wanted to set these people straight, but she didn't dare. It would bring just the sort of attention to herself that would most distress her mother. And it would not help his cause in the least. They would only say he had traded on her naïveté and kindness. But she was furious nonetheless. How could they be so angry at Hugh? How could they not understand?

He looked over at her, and then deliberately looked away. She ought to have expected it, but still it hurt. Rebecca felt a roaring in her ears and she reached out to grasp her sister's arm for fear she would faint. Now Penelope saw him and she went pale as well.

"My heavens! There is our Hugh," Penelope whispered to Rebecca, who had confided everything.

She did not trust herself to speak. Instead, Rebecca nodded.

"I wonder what Mama and Papa and Aunt Ariana will say when they realize he is here."

They already had. Lady Brisbane was viewing Hugh through narrowed but appreciative eyes and Lady Westcott was murmuring to herself, "Rowland is quite, quite wealthy. And he does seem most interested in our dear Rebecca."

Lord Westcott said nothing, but cleared his throat nervously. He had not told his wife what Rowland had said about that!

Even as they watched, the space around Hugh grew larger and larger as the *ton* made its decision to give him the cut direct.

Gradually both he and the Westcott party began to realize just how reviled he must be and he stopped, some distance away. He went very pale, then turned so they could not see his face. It seemed clear he meant to act as if he did not know them, as if they had never met.

Even Lady Westcott ceased to speculate upon his fortune and began to murmur, "Perhaps it would be best if he did not court our Rebecca, after all."

"If this is how the *ton* is going to react, it would be best indeed," Lord Westcott agreed. "A pity, but there it is. Can't have our Rebecca spurned because of him. The devil take it, I never thought they would be this angry at the man!"

When even her own parents turned their backs on Hugh, Rebecca could bear it no longer. She would not let these people hurt him. Not if there was anything she could do to stop it.

Rebecca grasped her fan so tightly that it snapped. Suddenly she threw it to the floor and began to march across the way to where Hugh stood all alone. She reached him just as the band struck up a waltz.

She should not do this, she knew. It would be fatal to waltz before the patronesses of Almack's gave her permission. But what sort of person would she be if she allowed this all to just happen? She had to do something.

Rebecca came to a halt directly before Hugh and when he tried to turn away she stepped to the side and forestalled him. In a loud voice she said, "This is the dance I promised you, I believe."

He tried to be kind. He tried to send her away. "I believe you are mistaken," he countered, and turned again.

Again Rebecca stepped to the side and in front of him. "I am not," she replied.

He looked down at her and Rebecca could read the agony in his eyes. For a long moment, matters hung in the balance. With her eyes, she told him it would be worse if he tried to walk away from her. Just when she was certain she had failed, he groaned and offered her his arm and led her to the dance floor.

Murmurs followed them. Vaguely, out of the corner of her eye, Rebecca was aware that her mother and father were glaring in her direction. Aunt Ariana was pale with dismay and even Penelope seemed not to approve.

But it didn't matter. Rebecca stepped into Hugh's arms

and together they began to waltz. The buzz of voices rose around them and one by one the other dancers fell away until it was only the two of them.

"Liar!" she said softly. "You said you didn't know how to dance."

"I said I didn't know how to dance well or gracefully," he countered.

Rebecca could feel his hand tremble on her back as her own trembled inside of his. But it didn't matter. Her back was straight and she would prove to him, and to the world, that at least one person did not disdain Hugh.

"It will all come about," she said, wishing she could stroke away the anxious lines in his face, lines that she knew were from concern on her behalf.

"I don't think so," he said. Then he smiled, a wry, bitter smile, and added, "I tried to warn you, you know. I am not fit company for any lady."

As the dance came to an end, Rebecca stared up at Hugh. His face was very pale and she could read the agony in his eyes. They seemed to be trying to apologize to her, as if he had anything to apologize for! She wanted to tell him so, indignantly. But before she could speak, he let go of her and stalked away, headed straight for the door.

Rebecca wanted to follow, but she could not. It would have done more harm than good. Instead, her back ramrod straight, she walked back to her parents and Aunt Ariana. The crowd parted for her as they had, before, for Hugh. Around her she could hear the murmurs of pity.

"More heart than sense."

"Foolish Westcott girl!"

"I wouldn't let my daughter behave so imprudently!"

Rebecca pretended she heard nothing. She moved, head held high, with dignity. When she reached her family she found Lady Westcott moaning. Lady Brisbane stood over her, waving a fan frantically. Penelope and her father both stood silent, with fatalistic expressions, as though waiting for the next disaster to befall.

The moment Rebecca reached her side, Lady Westcott reached out and grasped her daughter's hand. "We are going home now," she said, her voice a trifle shrill. "I have the headache. You have the headache. We all have the headache."

Rebecca did not protest. If Hugh were leaving, what point was there for her to remain?

Instinctively, her eyes went to where he was. And as she watched, a gentleman stepped out of the crowd and into Hugh's path. Rebecca did not know him but others did and there was a murmur of surprise. Apparently the man was very well respected on his own. And then another gentleman stepped forward, someone who had danced with Rebecca at a number of balls. And then a third.

It would be too much to say that everyone crowded forward, but gradually a few others did speak with Hugh. One or two ladies even danced with him, though not a waltz. And this time the other dancers stayed on the floor.

Rebecca stood transfixed, watching all of this. Once Hugh's resurrection had begun, her parents did not dare leave the ball. Not until they knew the outcome of the evening.

So Rebecca was able to watch, with a mixture of pride and jealousy, Hugh's partial redemption in the eyes of the *ton.* Still, he did not speak to her again, nor ask her to dance.

Rebecca tried to tell herself he was thinking of her, that he did not wish to risk additional censure for her. But it was not good enough. He should have known, she thought, that she would not have cared, if only he had come to her again.

All of the parties, it might be said, left Lady Merri-weather's ball with very mixed feelings about the evening. To be sure, Rowland's acceptance was an excellent sign, but no one could be pleased that Rebecca had made herself so conspicuous. Except Rebecca.

She knew what she had done for Hugh and she felt only pride. All would be well now, she was certain of it. But then, she didn't know that the worst rumor of all had not been spoken yet.

Chapter 17

Rebecca was not content to leave things as they were. How could she be, when Hugh needed her? But she knew it would be difficult. And so she planned her campaign as carefully as any general might have done. She listened to every word spoken about Hugh Rowland. She collected every scrap of information that she could.

She had already decided that she would not let propriety and pride stand between them, so she wrote to Hugh, asking him to call. He wrote back that he would not. It seemed he feared that because not everyone in the *ton* accepted what he had done, he would taint her by being seen in her company.

Rebecca read the note, then crumpled it in her hand. She wanted to throw it as hard as she could against the wall. Instead, she smoothed it out again, tears dropping onto the parchment as she did so.

She cried for every harsh word Hugh would hear without her to take the sting away. She cried because he thought he had to face the anger of the *ton* alone. She cried because he was building a wall around himself that she was very much afraid she could never overcome.

She tried to be angry. How dare he write a cold, proper note like this and thank her so formally? As though she had lent him a book or poured him a cup of tea or something equally prim and proper and utterly impersonal.

But it didn't work. No matter how angry she tried to be,

Rebecca kept worrying about Hugh. With her finger, she traced the letters of his writing, skipping over only those spots where her tears had caused the ink to run. He had such elegant penmanship. Certainly far nicer than her own. She rarely had the patience to write as neatly as this.

She lifted the paper and smelled it, hoping to catch just a hint of his scent. For she knew what Hugh, the pickpocket and vagabond, reeked of, but not what Mr. Rowland the gentleman might wear. And she had been too distracted yesterday to notice.

Rebecca found herself wondering what he ate, what he liked to wear, and everything else about the man. When he was a thief she had wanted to help him. Now that he was a gentleman she discovered, in the depths of her treacherous heart, that she wanted far more.

Her lower lip began to tremble. Thank heavens no one was here to see! Tears spilled down Rebecca's cheeks again and she made herself a vow. Somehow she was going to see Hugh again. Yes, and tell him once more how she felt.

And if he sent her away because he truly did not care for her, then so be it, Rebecca thought, tilting up her chin in her habitual gesture of defiance. It would be better to know the truth than to mope, hoping that something would come about. Better to know that she had been foolishly wrong about his feelings for her, than to waste her time hoping otherwise. Better to get on with her life. Though how she was going to do that if he didn't care was beyond her.

It took time to make her plans. Rebecca would have gone to see her brother-in-law, Lord Farrington, except that he had suddenly gone out of town. But surely someone else must know something about Mr. Rowland, the only question was who.

By dint of pretending to be suspicious of his sudden respectability, Rebecca was able to get her father to divulge Sir Parker's name.

"Though mind, not a word to anyone that he was involved," Lord Westcott warned her. "I collect Sir Parker works quite secretly and he would not appreciate it if anyone were to speak of this aloud."

"Oh, I shan't, Papa," Rebecca assured the earl fervently.

And she meant it. She had no wish to bruit about Sir Parker's role in anything. She only wished to go and see him. Since she was quite certain, however, that everyone would agree she could not call upon an unmarried gentleman on her own, she did not tell anyone what she meant to do. Or ask permission. She merely dragooned her abigail and set out to hire a hack to carry her there.

Sir Parker could not be said to be overjoyed to see Lady Rebecca. He greeted her calmly, however, and bade her be seated. He took a chair opposite and regarded her from beneath hooded lids.

"You are no doubt wondering why I am here," she said, leaning forward. "And worried as to what I might know. But I assure you I mean to keep your secret. I only wish to speak to you about Mr. Rowland."

"Mr. Rowland?" Sir Parker echoed faintly. "Do I know the man? The name seems faintly familiar. Ah, yes, he is somehow mixed up in this dreadful scandal involving thieves and gentlemen, is he not?"

Rebecca regarded him scathingly as she said, "I have already wormed out of my father the knowledge of your letter on Hugh's behalf so you needn't keep up such a pretense of innocence with me. Recollect that I have also already told you I mean to keep your secret."

He pursed his lips. "Suppose we pretend, and I concede nothing, you understand, that I know Mr. Rowland. Why do you come to me? What is it you wish me to do?"

"I wish you to tell me all about him," Rebecca said earnestly. "I wish to know why he is so adamantly opposed to marriage! I know I am putting myself beyond the pale by admitting to you, a stranger, my concern for him, but I cannot help it! He needs me, I know it, and he simply won't admit it."

"Perhaps he fancies a different sort of female," Sir Parker said carelessly. "Or none."

It was possible. A sensible reply. And yet Rebecca could not accept it. She gave a most unladylike snort. "He cares for me, I know he does. And yet he seems determined not to marry. I want to know why."

"Why?" Sir Parker asked, leaning forward himself. "Why do you care? Because your pride is injured? Because you conceive yourself to have a broken heart?"

Rebecca felt her heart twist. "Both those things," she admitted. "But even more, I wish to know because of Hugh. Because of the unhappiness I saw in his eyes when he spoke of marriage. He has been hurt, dreadfully, I am sure. And I want to help him, if I can. Even if it means that, in the end, he marries someone else."

For a long moment, Sir Parker was silent. Then, slowly, he nodded. "I do believe I shall help you. Mind," he said, holding up a hand at her small cry of triumph, "I don't know the circumstances either. I can only try to discover them, and it is not at all certain that Hugh will tell me. Or that you will like the answer. Still, I will try. If I am successful, I shall come and take you out for a ride in my carriage. You are not," he said severely, "to come here again."

"I won't," Rebecca said meekly.

Sir Parker wisely looked as though he did not entirely believe her. But she meant it. She would not come here again. Unless, of course, too much time passed and she didn't have a choice.

Hugh, arriving some time later, had no warning as to the grilling he was about to endure. It was delicately done. So delicately that he scarcely knew what Sir Parker was about.

Hugh complained about the ingratitude of the *ton* for his having helped to protect it.

"You'd best learn now that they are never grateful," Sir Parker said, with some amusement. "This censure will pass when a new scandal rises to take its place."

Hugh rose to his feet and stalked over to the fireplace where he stared down into the cold grate. "I wish I could be so certain," he said sardonically. "What I should like to know is why they cannot understand now."

"Because they don't wish to understand. Because they don't wish to believe that someone they liked, someone they entertained in their homes, could be capable of evil. They would rather believe it of someone they dislike or who is of a different class," Sir Parker said heavily. "Come, it has never bothered you before, what anyone thought of you. Why should you begin to care now?"

"Because of Lady Rebecca, the Earl of Westcott's daughter. They are blaming her for taking up my cause," Hugh said, without looking up. "I do not care so much for myself, but I do not wish to see her obliged to endure the censure of society."

"Ah. I see."

Hugh was not deceived. He lifted his head and smiled ruefully at Sir Parker. "No, you do not," he said curtly.

"Then tell me."

"There is nothing to tell," Hugh said with a shrug, looking back down at the fireplace.

"Not even that you mean to court the girl?"

That got Rowland's attention. He looked at Sir Parker through narrowed eyes. "I do not mean to do so," he countered forcefully.

"Why not?" Sir Parker asked with all apparent innocence. "Do you not like the girl?"

"Too much," Hugh said, his voice rueful again, "to allow her to share my life. Or to suffer the wagging tongues of the *ton*."

"Poppycock!" Sir Parker exploded. "You are the most arrogant young puppy I have ever seen! How dare you presume to decide for Lady Rebecca what is best for her? Do you think her one of those empty-headed sorts of chits who haven't two thoughts to rub together?"

"Good God, no!" Hugh exclaimed, startled.

"Then grant her the respect to believe she is capable of knowing her own mind," Sir Parker said scornfully.

But that was going too far. Hugh drew himself up to his full height and said, frostily, "It is much more complicated than that, though you will persist in pretending to misunderstand. Lady Rebecca would feel she must stand by me, as she did last night, whatever the cost to herself."

Sir Parker snorted and rose to his feet. "Poppycock!" he repeated. "I suppose there is no reasoning with you. But if you wish to protect her, do not hide. That would be fatal. It would make people think you had a reason to do so. Show yourself everywhere! Go for a ride in the park!"

Hugh shook his head, but he went. It would do him good, he decided, and could do no possible harm. In any event, he had no inclination to hide. He had done nothing to apologize for and he would not act as if he had.

Rebecca read the note from Sir Parker the moment it arrived. She grinned. It was not very difficult for Rebecca to persuade Miss Tibbles to go to the park with her and Penelope, for the governess was a strong believer in the benefits of exercise. That did not mean she was without her suspicions.

"Why that park and not another?" Miss Tibbles asked bluntly when Rebecca ventured to suggest where they should go.

Rebecca tried to look innocent. "Everyone goes there and we may see any number of acquaintances," she said meekly.

"She hopes to see Mr. Rowland," Penelope said with a sniff. "And I, for one, hope she does not."

Miss Tibbles pondered this piece of information which,

in truth, did not surprise her. She had heard all about Mr. Rowland's visit yesterday and the fact that he was the same person as the servant Hugh. She also knew that at the moment he was *persona non grata* with many of the *ton* and that he had told both Lord Westcott and Rebecca that he was not hanging out for a wife.

The trouble was, Miss Tibbles liked Hugh. And therein lay her dilemma. As if she could read her governess's mind, Rebecca said, "Surely it can do no harm to go for a walk in the park? One would not wish the *ton* to believe I thought I ought to hide."

Miss Tibbles fairly bristled at the notion. "Indeed not!" she exclaimed. "Very well. We shall go to the park. Mind, I expect you to be on your very best behavior, Rebecca! We shall do nothing to give the *ton* even more to gossip about. Let someone else become the subject of their latest *on-dits*."

"Yes, Miss Tibbles."

And indeed, Rebecca did not mean to cause trouble. She merely hoped to catch a glimpse of Hugh, or Mr. Rowland as she must now learn to call him. Failing that, she hoped that some acquaintance, maliciously or otherwise, would give her some notion of his direction. She did not in the least plan what was about to happen.

Still, when she saw him, she could not help herself. She looked directly at Hugh and smiled. He made as if to turn his horse the other way, to go in the opposite direction of Rebecca and her party. And she could not allow that to happen, could she?

The next thing anyone knew, Rebecca was dashing toward Hugh, ignoring Miss Tibbles's cry of distress behind her. Hugh's horse shied at this unseemly behavior and he had to yank hard on the reins to keep from trampling her. In an instant he was off his horse and reaching out to shake her.

At least, that was what Rebecca thought he meant to do.

And behind her, she could hear Miss Tibbles clear her throat in an ominous way. Any moment a peal would be rung over both their heads and all chance to talk to Hugh would be gone.

Without considering any of the possible repercussions, Rebecca closed her eyes, moaned loudly, and pitched forward, into Hugh's arms as though she had just fainted.

Cursing both loudly and under his breath, Hugh caught Rebecca. She had to be pretending, he told himself angrily, and if he had his way, someone would teach her a good stern lesson about such nonsense.

But what if she wasn't pretending. Certainly, she lay very pale in his arms. And her lashes rested against her cheeks without even fluttering. What if something really was wrong with her?

Hugh felt an unexpected pang of alarm at the thought. He wanted to chafe her hands, speak to her urgently, he wanted to kiss her hands, her cheeks, her lips. Anything to bring her awake again.

And he could do none of those things. Not with so many people watching. One of them called out, a broad grin upon his face, "Careful, Rowland, or you'll find yourself forced to marry the girl!"

"Nonsense, sir!" Miss Tibbles weighed in heavily. "And I'll thank you not to make matters worse by saying such things aloud."

"Rebecca isn't going to marry anyone," Penelope said stoutly. "Neither of us ever will. And anyone who says otherwise is a liar."

Hugh heard none of it. His attention was entirely focused on Rebecca. He wanted to shout at her. He wanted to hold her close. He wanted, dear God, as foolish as it seemed, he wanted to love her. But, for her sake, he could not let himself commit such folly. And right now, the last thing he must let her do was try to make a spectacle of herself to force his hand.

Carefully, he tilted Lady Rebecca until she was all but standing upright. Then Rowland set her on her feet, trusting that she was playacting and would stop the moment she had no choice.

And he was right. As her feet touched the ground, her eyes snapped open and she said, softly, "Coward!"

But Hugh had himself well in hand again. He took a step back from her, brushed some imaginary dirt off his jacket, and said, coolly, "Your servant, my lady. You'd best see a doctor about these fainting fits."

The change in her expression was comical. Or would have been if Hugh hadn't been so certain her heart was breaking. He could see the tears begin to gather at the corners of her eyes and the way she bravely dashed them aside.

She sniffed, tilted up her head, and said to her companions, "Come along, we don't wish to dawdle here. Not if some people do not wish our company."

Hugh watched them go, feeling oddly bereft. Only when they were some distance away did he reluctantly mount his horse again. As quickly as he could, without exciting further comment, he left the park and returned to visit Sir Parker and told him what had taken place.

"Why the devil can't she be sensible about all this?" Hugh demanded, drinking the brandy Sir Parker had offered him.

"Why should she be?" Sir Parker countered, clearly enjoying himself. "Her older sisters, by all accounts, have found great happiness by flouting convention. Why should she not believe she can do the same?"

"But I don't wish to marry her," Hugh complained.

"Don't you?" Sir Parker asked softly.

Now Rowland laughed. "You are a fine one to talk, sir! You are quite a few years older than I and you have never stepped into the parson's trap. How dare you lecture me on the subject?"

Not in the least disconcerted, Sir Parker smiled kindly and replied, "Perhaps because I have a fondness for you, my boy. And for her ladyship."

Hugh snorted in disbelief.

In the same good-natured vein as before, Sir Parker said, "There is a book you ought to read. It might do you some good."

"A book?" Hugh echoed warily.

"It's called *Pride and Prejudice*. I shall lend you a copy."

"It is not a case of too much pride as too little," Hugh protested, affronted.

Sir Parker shook his head. "That is what you may think," he said, "but I assure you I, and I suspect, Lady Rebecca, know far better."

Hugh merely stared at him, his face set in stone, and after a moment Sir Parker said gently, "All right. You say that I don't understand. Perhaps you are right. If so, then tell me. Why are you so averse to courting Westcott's daughter?"

For a long moment, Hugh did not answer and Sir Parker had almost decided he never would when Rowland began to speak.

"All my life I have been surrounded by married couples who were fighting. It is not a picture I want for myself. I will not make myself and some hapless female, particularly not Lady Rebecca, unhappy by repeating such a pattern!"

"What makes you so certain you will?" Sir Parker objected.

"Because," Hugh said, not troubling to hide the bleakness in his eyes, "it is the only pattern I know. And because I did so with Felicity Hamilton. She called me an overbearing tyrant. And she was right. She also called me a clumsy fool. And she was right about that, as well. And since then I have done nothing to improve my nature. Come sir, admit it. I am no fit partner for any delicately bred young lady!"

Hugh paused and waited. Sir Parker's response was not in the least what he expected.

"Poppycock! Read the book and think about it, and think about Lady Rebecca, and then decide if you still mean to be a damn fool!"

Chapter 18

Her actions in the park had not, perhaps, been the wisest thing she could have done, Rebecca thought. They had resulted in a thundering scold from Miss Tibbles the moment the three reached home. And another thundering scold once her mother and aunt heard about it from their friends.

Indeed, so incensed and alarmed were her family that for the next few days Rebecca found herself closely guarded as they tried to protect her from any possible contact with Mr. Hugh Rowland.

Fortunately, only Papa knew of the connection between Sir Parker and Hugh. And he happened to be out when that gentleman came to call so that she and Penelope were allowed to accept his invitation to go for a drive in the park. Rebecca sent up a tiny, silent prayer of thanks that her father was not inclined to be overly forthcoming with his family.

Sir Parker played the role of potential suitor perfectly and it was with a fond smile that Lady Westcott watched him hand her daughters into his carriage. He maintained this pose just so long as it took to reach the park. Then, as he tooled his carriage neatly around, he let Rebecca come straight to the point.

"Why is he so determined to stay away from me?" she asked plaintively. "I only wish to help."

"He believes himself to be too clumsy and boorish to suit any lady. He believes it his duty," Sir Parker said carefully, "to protect you from censure and unhappiness."

Rebecca muttered an oath she hadn't known she knew, then promptly colored up. Penelope gasped in protest, and both looked at Sir Parker to see how he had taken this most unladylike behavior.

"Think nothing of it," he said, with a distinct twinkle in his eyes. "I quite agree, you know. Told him you weren't made of such fragile stuff, but he won't listen to me."

"Well, one way or another he shall listen to me," Rebecca said stoutly, a martial glint in her eye.

Sir Parker grinned. "I shall be most interested to see what success you have."

Rebecca grinned back at him. "Good, for I may need your help. Please tell me everything you know about Mr. Rowland and his family."

Nothing loath, Sir Parker was happy to oblige. He liked Lady Rebecca and he liked Hugh and nothing would make him happier than to see the pair together. He concluded, however, by warning her, "No playing tricks on him, now, m'lady. Hugh is not the man to tolerate such things. He is plain-spoken and likes those about him to be plain-spoken as well."

Rebecca jutted out her chin. "I shouldn't think of such a thing," she answered. "I simply mean to make him aware that I don't need such protection and that he has to stop."

Sir Parker chuckled.

He was still laughing as he drew his carriage to a halt in front of Lady Brisbane's townhouse. And there they all saw Hugh waiting on the steps, patently in a towering rage.

Hugh had read the book Sir Parker gave him. And while he could not say that he believed it applied to him, he found it interesting.

He had also pondered Sir Parker's words and even managed to persuade himself that while he did not agree with him, it might still be a wise notion to explain matters more completely to Lady Rebecca.

Perhaps, he persuaded himself, he had been a trifle hasty. After all, she did deserve a certain courtesy from him for having tried so hard to help him when he was masquerading as a thief. Besides, after his experience in the park, he did not wish to discover what she would do if he did not call upon her. It was clearly his duty to prevent any further folly on her part.

So Hugh had nerved himself to call once more at Lady Brisbane's townhouse. He came at an unfashionably early hour, hoping she would not yet be surrounded by other callers. There he had met with a facer.

"Lady Rebecca is not at home," Jeffries said frostily, careful to look at the ceiling so that he need not meet Hugh's eyes. "I collect she went out for a drive with a gentleman. A Sir Parker."

"Sir Parker?" Hugh exploded.

"Yes, sir. I collect he invited Lady Rebecca and her sister, Lady Penelope, for a drive around the park," Jeffries explained. "They left some time ago."

And then the major domo closed the door without asking if he wished to wait. Hugh could not blame the fellow. He would not like to think he had been tricked in such a way either.

As Hugh went back down the steps, he found himself wondering just what Sir Parker was up to. He had a strong suspicion the older gentleman was playing matchmaker and at the moment Hugh was not inclined to appreciate such interference in his life.

He met Lord Westcott coming up the steps, and the meeting proved most awkward. The earl glared at Hugh and Hugh stared evenly back.

"I came," he said, "to explain to your daughter why I will not come to see her again."

Westcott nodded. "Good. Though you might have just sent around a note. No," he amended, holding up a hand, "I

collect you tried that already. With disastrous conse-
quences, I have heard."

He paused, looked at Hugh with a great deal of unease,
and then finally blurted out, "They are saying you did away
with Philip Caldwell. That you are responsible for his dis-
appearance. Is it true?"

A sudden inspiration occurred to Hugh. Here was a way
to convince Lady Rebecca, and her family, once and for all,
that he was no fit mate for her. If she believed him, if her
family believed he was guilty of the charge against him,
surely they would make certain she did not try to see him
again? Granted, once Farrington returned to London with
Caldwell in tow, the truth would come out, but perhaps by
then Lady Rebecca would have fixed her interest on someone else.

He tilted up his chin, made his voice cool and insolent,
and half turned away as he answered, "Yes, it is."

And if an unholy gleam of triumph lit his eyes, Lord
Westcott did not see it.

"Then damn you, sir," the earl replied, "I wish you never
to speak to my daughter again!"

Lord Westcott then turned his back and slammed the
door behind him as he entered the house. Hugh had just
reached the bottom of the steps when Sir Parker's carriage
neatly pulled to a halt right in front of him. And the man,
blast his soul, was laughing!

Hugh didn't stop to consider the wisdom of his actions.
He stepped forward, put a hand on the carriage, and demanded, "What the devil is going on here?"

Sir Parker looked at him and, with wide, innocent eyes,
said blandly, "I have heard so much about the Earl of Westcott's lovely daughters that I had to come and see them for
myself. And I must say, Rowland, they are even more en-
chanting than I imagined."

Penelope grimaced, but Hugh would have sworn Rebecca was trying very hard to suppress laughter of her own.

"You've no interest in dallying after the ladies," he said through clenched teeth.

Sir Parker shrugged. "A man may change."

"Not ladies this young," Hugh persisted.

Again Sir Parker grinned. "A man may change," he repeated.

Then, apparently having decided he had not baited Hugh sufficiently, he tossed the reins to his tiger and helped the ladies down.

"I had a delightful time," he said, bowing to both of them, "and I very much hope we may be able to do this again. I cannot recall the last time I have had so much fun."

There was no arguing with the man. He would only find a way to irritate Rowland further. Hugh turned on his heel and started to walk away.

"What? Don't you mean to come in and call upon the ladies?" Sir Parker called after him.

"I am no fit company for a ladies' drawing room," Hugh said, deliberately avoiding Lady Rebecca's eyes. "I've no social graces and would only embarrass everyone."

Then she almost undid him. She laid a gentle hand on his arm and looked up at him earnestly as she said softly, "I shouldn't care."

Because it was so tempting, because he wanted so much to believe her, Hugh made himself pull his arm roughly away. And he spoke harshly as he said, "Perhaps I do."

But he still could not daunt her. She shook her head sadly, but her voice was gentle as she replied, "You cannot put me off that way, Hugh. I know you to be a good and honorable and wonderful man."

The words sent a shiver of panic through him. He almost believed her. And that would be fatal—to begin to believe that he could find love and happiness. But no, if he tried, he would only disappoint her and himself. And in the end their parting would be as bitter as when Felicity had flung his ring back in his face and married another man.

He could not do that to Lady Rebecca and so he drawled, "Indeed? But then you are remarkably naive. Haven't you heard? I murdered Philip Caldwell."

And then he walked away.

Even without turning to look, Hugh knew he had left three stunned people staring open-mouthed after him. Another man might have been daunted. Hugh acquired a spring to his step, and he felt better than he had for some time.

Her head in a whirl, Rebecca turned to Sir Parker and looked at him helplessly. He looked as distressed as she felt.

"Oh, dear!" he said. "If that is the tack Rowland means to take, the cat *will* be among the pigeons."

"It isn't true, is it?" Rebecca asked, her face very pale.

Sir Parker quirked an eyebrow at her. "Whether it is or not, if Rowland means to go about saying so, then we are all in the suds. I shall do my best to help him, of course, but it won't be easy." He paused then asked, "Daunted yet?"

Rebecca looked up at him. She jutted forward her chin and said, "Not a bit of it!"

With patent amusement, Sir Parker saluted her and watched as both ladies mounted the steps of the townhouse. He was chuckling as he drove away. There were few things, he thought, that could prove more amusing than watching Lady Rebecca and Hugh Rowland at loggerheads.

Inside the house, Rebecca went in search of her mother. Sir Parker had told her the events to which Hugh might be invited, and those which he was most likely to accept. Now she had to persuade her mother to agree to attend them as well. Which shouldn't be difficult, as Lady Westcott was most anxious to puff off her daughters everywhere she could and was happy to take them to any social affair they were willing to attend.

Lord Westcott, however, for once was perspicacious

enough to realize something was amiss. He found a moment when Rebecca was alone and asked her point blank, "Rowland, is it?"

Her flushed cheeks were apparently answer enough, for he sighed and tried to reason with her.

"Come now, Rebecca, Rowland is said to have killed a fellow! You cannot wish for a connection with him, knowing that?"

Rebecca took a deep breath. "I do not believe it of him," she said stubbornly. "I know he is, he must be, innocent of the charge."

"Then let him prove it. When he does and the *ton* ceases to snub him, he may call upon you again. If he wishes to. I thought he made it deuced clear he was not hanging out for a wife.

"Mind, I liked Mr. Rowland," the earl went on. "He had the decency to tell me that he knew his name mustn't be linked with yours. And he is quite right, at least not until all this is settled. Though how it can be when he admits to doing in young Caldwell, I cannot imagine."

"He did not, could not, have harmed the man," Rebecca repeated stubbornly.

Lord Westcott sighed. "Admitted it himself. Didn't try to justify it, either. Maybe it was self-defense. I don't know. But if he don't choose to say so, then it don't change things at all."

"Oh, yes," Rebecca said mutinously, "it does."

Chapter 19

The Westcotts, Lady Brisbane, and most of the *ton* did not know what to think. There were rumors and counter rumors everywhere. And Hugh Rowland became a social success.

The *ton* might be unhappy with Mr. Hugh Rowland. The *ton* might blame him for what was happening to their sons and brothers. The *ton* might even wonder what he had done with Philip Caldwell, though Sir Parker did his best to scotch those rumors. But Hugh Rowland was a sensation, and many hostesses were determined to have him at their social affairs.

It was, after all, so deliciously exciting. Particularly with the added piquancy of watching the Earl of Westcott's daughter in determined pursuit of the man. And it was even more amusing to see his useless attempts to stay out of her way.

Rebecca decided that her first point of attack would be to prove to Hugh that he was not as clumsy or ham-fisted as he claimed to be. That he was indeed up to snuff and could not flummox her into believing otherwise. And the way to do that, she decided, was to treat him precisely as if she had taken him at his word in the matter. The question of Philip Caldwell, she thought darkly, she would resolve later, when he was finally willing to tell her the truth.

At every opportunity, when she encountered Hugh in public, Rebecca would helpfully point out to him just how he ought to go on. Her family was helpless to stop her without either creating an even more outrageous scene or spiriting her away from London—either of which would have caused even more gossip.

So Rebecca did as she wished. She would tell Hugh, if they happened to be seated near one another, and hostesses soon decided it would be most amusing to arrange it so, which fork to use, and when to use his napkin.

If there was dancing, she would, to the horror of her family, attempt to tell him who he ought to ask to dance and remind him of the steps to the pattern. She was very eager to please, and could not understand why Mr. Rowland did not appear grateful for her help.

With some exasperation, he finally told her that he knew quite well which fork to use, thank you very much, and she could refrain from trying to tell him how to manage a morning call or a country dance, because he had mastered the rules already.

This contretemps occurred in the middle of Almack's and Lady Westcott promptly fumbled for her smelling salts. Rebecca, however, hid her smile of satisfaction as she said, quite meekly, "How very foolish of me, Mr. Rowland. Clearly you are far more conversant with the rules of propriety than I realized. It was your talk of being a country bumpkin that misled me."

He ought to have swallowed his pride and let her advise him. Anyone could see that he was trying to do so. But in the end he could not. He was not, Rebecca thought, a man who was accustomed to being told what to do.

The rest of the *ton* naturally watched this process with great fascination. There were bets laid at White's, though not in Mr. Rowland's hearing, and friendly wagers placed among the ladies as well. And of course the true romantics in the *ton* kept hoping the two would make a match of it and bother what anyone said. They were sure the *on-dits* about Rowland and Caldwell were a farrago of nonsense, for otherwise the police would surely have arrested him, and they didn't want to hear another word about it.

Once the issue of his competence in society was settled, Rebecca decided to corner Hugh and ask him directly about Caldwell. She managed to do so at Lady Jersey's ball.

He tried to evade the point, tried to use it as an excuse to quarrel. She refused. He tried to tell her that she was a fool. She lost patience and scolded him roundly.

"You cannot persuade me you harmed anyone except out of direst need!" she said.

"No? You seem to have a highly inflated opinion of my character," he said coolly.

She snorted. "I have no such thing! I know very well you are a pig-headed, arrogant idiot."

He looked distinctly taken aback and none too pleased by this evaluation of his character. Rebecca advanced upon him and pressed her point.

"You think to make me believe the worst of you. Well, I won't. I still have the box you made for my cat and her kittens, the home you made for my bird. You cannot tell me those were the products of a villain's hands."

"You rescue too many things," he muttered, retreating further. "But I am no longer one of your pet projects in need of such."

"No?" Rebecca took a step toward him. With a sigh, she reached out and touched his cheek, for the briefest of moments. Then, because she could see it distressed him, she drew back.

"I think you need me more than ever," she said softly. "I think you believe yourself such a horrid wretch you have no right to love or happiness."

"On the contrary," he retorted, feeling himself on stronger ground, "I do think I have a right to happiness, and that is why I refuse to saddle myself with a wife."

"Was your parents' marriage so very horrid then?" she asked with a sympathy in her voice that almost undid him.

"It is not always so. Think of my parents. They have been happy together. And so were my aunt and Lord Brisbane. I could take you to see my sisters and their husbands. They are all happy as well."

He was shaken. She could see it. But then someone came to claim her hand for a dance, putting an end to the tête-à-tête, and she was swept away from him. He swiftly made good his escape.

And so it might have gone on and on had Lord Halifax not escaped from prison.

Halifax was in the foulest of moods. He did not like prison, even though his wealth ameliorated much of the situation for him. Nor did he fancy swinging from the end of a rope, which was the inevitable future for him if he did not escape.

Halifax placed the blame squarely where he thought it belonged. On Hugh Rowland. And he thought he knew just how to hurt the man. He would strike at Lady Rebecca. Even in prison he had heard what was happening between the two, and for all Mr. Hugh Rowland pretended indifference to the girl, Halifax was certain he knew better.

He kept remembering his sister's ball and the stranger who he now knew must have been Rowland. Oh, yes, Rowland would pay. And so would the proud lady who had done so much to help him.

Rebecca was puzzled but rather pleased when she received Hugh's note asking her to meet him at the park. Perhaps he had finally come to his senses.

To be sure, his writing seemed more shaky than before, but the other note he had sent her was so crumpled and smeared with her tears that it was very difficult to compare the two missives.

Perhaps the agitation betrayed by the handwriting in this note was because he meant, finally, to declare his feelings for her! Either that or he meant to be more difficult still, she thought darkly.

Well, either way, he had asked to see her and surely that must be an excellent sign. In any case, Rebecca wished to ask him about a lady named Felicity Hamilton. Her name had been mentioned, once or twice, with significant glances cast in her direction. Perhaps, she thought with a pang, she was the reason he was so determined to turn Rebecca away.

Her eyes sparkling with anticipation, Rebecca dressed with particular care and fairly burbled with happiness as she set out with Penelope in tow. Her twin was more skeptical, but even she, by now, had decided that if Rebecca's heart was set on Mr. Rowland, then Mr. Rowland she should have.

Hugh cursed softly under his breath when he read Lady Rebecca's message. So she wished to meet him, did she? It was nonsense, all nonsense. No doubt she still hoped to bring him up to scratch and this was more of her plan. Why did she think he would come this time, when he had not come before? And why ask him to meet her in the park?

He almost tossed the note into the fireplace, but at the last moment changed his mind. Very well, he would go and try once more to talk her out of her folly. He wished he could believe that in a public park there would be some constraints to her behavior. Unfortunately, after recent events he was not in the least certain of any such thing.

Miss Tibbles tapped her chin thoughtfully. It was not like Rebecca and Penelope to go out for a walk at this time of day. And certainly not without telling her. To be sure, they had taken a footman, but even that was suspect. Something was definitely odd here.

With a purposeful gleam in her eyes she went straight to the twins' bedroom and began to look about for something,

anything, that might explain this strange start. It did not
take very long to find it.

Miss Tibbles sighed. She was tempted not to intervene.
She was growing so very tired of this nonsense and she did
not really think Mr. Rowland would go beyond the line.
Not in such a public place, and not with Penelope present.
Why, if he tried, Miss Tibbles had no doubt that Penelope
would instantly put him in his place.

But it would not do, of course. However tired she might
be, Miss Tibbles knew her duty. It was not Mr. Rowland's
behavior she must fear, but the impulsiveness of her own
charge, Rebecca. With another sigh, this time one of resig-
nation, she went to get her cloak.

Halifax had not counted on the presence of Lady Penelope, but he supposed he should have expected something of
the sort. Certainly he had taken the precaution of arranging
a little something to distract the servant he had expected to
accompany Lady Rebecca. Ah, well, he thought, how much
trouble could one extra girl be?

Rebecca looked around in confusion. There was no sign
of Mr. Rowland anywhere. Had she misunderstood the
day? The time? In her eagerness, had she arrived too early?
She wished she had thought to bring the note, but it was
back home under her pillow.

A commotion began nearby, and the footman turned to
look. At the same moment, Rebecca spotted Mr. Rowland
on the far side of the park. She had to cross the carriage
way, however, to reach him, right by a closed coach that
was stopped with the driver examining the wheel.

As Rebecca and Penelope drew alongside the coach, the
door suddenly opened, two men sprang out, and the next
thing she knew, they were both being bundled inside.

From a distance, as she fought her attacker, Rebecca
heard Mr. Rowland crying out her name. That was all she

could hear, however, for the coach door shut and the coach began moving, picking up speed at a shocking pace. She and Penelope scarcely had time to find seats opposite the other occupant of the coach before a sharp turn almost threw them to the floor.

"Lord Halifax!" Rebecca exclaimed.

He inclined his head politely. "The very same, ladies."

"You are supposed to be in prison," Penelope said with a frown.

His teeth showed as he smiled, but it was not a friendly smile; rather it seemed to Rebecca to be a most predatory one. "So I am," he agreed.

"Then what are you doing here, and why did you have your men attack us this way?" Rebecca demanded.

Halifax shrugged and spread his hands. "But how else was I to have my revenge?"

"You shouldn't," Penelope told him roundly. "You're a nasty man and I wish to go home at once."

"Alas," Halifax told her, "that is not possible. I need you, or rather your sister, as bait, you see."

"Bait for whom?" Rebecca asked warily, but it wasn't really a question. She was very much afraid she already knew. She was right.

"For Rowland, of course," Halifax said mockingly. "Couldn't you guess?"

"What makes you think he will come after me?" Rebecca asked with false bravado.

Halifax laughed, and the sound was a frightening one. "I may have been in prison, Lady Rebecca," he said softly, "but I am not dead. Word was brought to me of the latest *on-dits* and you and Rowland formed the basis of many of them. He'll come, my lady, never fear, he'll come."

Rebecca shivered. That was precisely what she feared. Still, she tried to brazen matters out. "And how is he supposed to find us? I suppose you have sent him directions?"

Halifax chuckled. "Better, my lady. I arranged for him to

be in the park to see you abducted. Rowland is a most resourceful man—as I have cause to know, to my deepest regret. He will find a way to follow us, oh, yes, I am certain
he will find a way."

"Papa is going to be very angry when he hears of this,"
Penelope told Halifax. "I dare say he might even call you
out. So you had best stop the coach and set us down right
now and let us go home before you get yourself into any
further trouble."

"Any further trouble?" Halifax echoed incredulously.
"Lady Penelope, I am already certain to swing from the
hangman's noose if they catch me. What more than that
could I possibly have to fear?"

There was nothing that could be said to that and Penelope became very quiet, huddled as she was in her corner of
the coach.

Rebecca, however, was not so easily cowed. She pretended to relax against the squabs as though she had not a
care in the world. But her mind was working furiously, trying to find some way out of this mess. For once she truly
regretted not telling Miss Tibbles what mischief she had
been getting into.

Miss Tibbles searched the park with dismay, particularly
once she discovered the footman standing about looking
bewildered.

"Patrick, what happened here?" she demanded severely.

"I don't know," he answered. "There was a fight and
when I turned around, the ladies, they was gone."

"Did you see nothing?" Miss Tibbles persisted.

"Nothing at all," he said, hanging his head.

Nor did Miss Tibbles see Mr. Rowland racing his own
curricle out through the gates of the park. Instead, after a
brief search, she sent the footman to Mr. Rowland's lodgings and herself headed as quickly as she could in the direction of Lady Brisbane's townhouse.

Chapter 20

Hugh clung to the reins as he drove his curricle through the crowded streets. Now he understood why the note asked him to bring it. Whoever had kidnapped Lady Rebecca, and he had no doubt that it was Lord Halifax who had done so, wished him to be able to follow. Clearly, Lady Rebecca had only been the bait for a very nasty trap.

Grimly, he wondered just what Halifax had planned for them. It could not be anything good. Hugh also cursed himself for ever allowing Lady Rebecca to come to Lord Halifax's attention. It was the worst disservice he could have done the girl. If only he had not saved her and she had not insisted on taking him home!

Hugh had never considered himself a particularly violent man. But right now the notion of putting his hands around Halifax's neck and squeezing as hard as he could seemed very appealing. At the very least he meant to plant him a facer as soon as he caught up with the carriage in front of him.

Halifax had chosen a coach that would be easy to follow—it sported bright blue panels and vivid yellow trim—so that even if Hugh had fallen behind, he would find it easy to discover where it had gone.

That did not bode well, Hugh thought. If only he had time to send for help. But of course he did!

Abruptly, he pulled his curricle to a halt and called over a young lad on the street. He gave him directions to Sir

Parker's house and made him memorize a brief message. A silver coin with the promise of more from Sir Parker sped the lad on his way.

Moments later, Hugh was on his own way in continued pursuit of Halifax. How fortunate that his lordship had gone to such pains to be sure Hugh would be able to follow. It appeared that he had counted on Hugh being so caught up in the chase that he would not pause to send for help.

The rattling coach came to a halt so abruptly that had Rebecca and Penelope not been holding onto the straps, they would have been thrown from their seats. Even Lord Halifax cursed the clumsiness of the coachman.

His first words, however, as the door was flung open was to demand if there were any other carriages in sight.

"No, m'lord. Not for some time," the coachman said, shaking his head.

"Perhaps Mr. Rowland decided he had better things to do than to follow you on this wild chase," Rebecca suggested with a calm she did not feel.

Halifax's eyes narrowed as he stared at her, but then his eyes fell on her trembling hands. "No," he said, a smile again crossing his face, "he will be here. He has just given us time to go indoors by his delay. Come, you will find everything already prepared for your arrival."

Both Rebecca and Penelope disdained the hands held out to help them down from the carriage. There was no way to escape, however. Not when two of Halifax's ruffians flanked them all the way to the front door of the mansion.

"One of your estates?" Rebecca hazarded, determined not to let Halifax see any more of her fear than she could help. "It does not seem in very good repair."

He laughed, but not kindly. "Mine? Oh, no, Lady Rebecca. I am not so foolish as that. No, this pile of stone belongs to one of my, er, associates. A young fellow with more hair than wit. I hear he is already on his way to America. Meanwhile, since he has no need for the place while he is gone, I am using it. And since he once bade me to treat it as my own, and told his servants as well, they do not dare question my right to do so."

If Rebecca thought their meekness was due more to the menace of Halifax's ruffians than to any orders issued by their misguided master, she did not say so aloud. Instead, as she stood at the top of the steps, in the brief moments before she and Penelope were hustled inside, she looked back to see if there were any sign of Mr. Rowland following. There was none, and she did not know whether to be pleased or displeased over that.

Halifax laughed again. "Your concern is quite touching, Lady Rebecca. Is it a concern for yourself or for Mr. Rowland?"

"Myself, of course," Rebecca said, tossing her head. "You are very foolish and insulting if you think I could care for an arrogant fellow like that!"

"You seem to have cared a great deal when you thought him a mere servant," Lord Halifax countered softly.

Rebecca sniffed. "As an inferior to be watched out for, of course I did so. It is the same with every other servant in my aunt's household. But as a man? A possible suitor? Preposterous!"

"And yet," Halifax said, his voice silky with danger, "it is said your pursuit of him has been most determined these past few weeks."

Rebecca shrugged. "It was amusing, nothing more. Had he actually been in danger of returning my attentions, it would have been quite different. But I knew I was safe. Mr. Rowland is a fool."

Penelope watched her sister doubtfully, but would not contradict her. At least not while Lord Halifax was watching. He smiled wolfishly.

"And of course I must believe whatever you tell me, Lady Rebecca," he said derisively.

A moment later he was showing the two girls into a small room that had been fixed with a stout door that locked from the outside.

"You will be a trifle cramped in here," he said, "but it will not be for long. I did not anticipate, you see, that you would bring your sister, Lady Rebecca, and I made provisions only for you."

"Oh, you plan to let us go soon?" Penelope asked brightly. "Perhaps when Mr. Rowland arrives?"

Halifax shook his head and his face took on a lugubrious expression. "No, my ladies," he said with a mock sigh, "I fear you will not be leaving this estate at all. But I will endeavor to make your deaths as swift and painless as possible. The same cannot be said for what I intend for Mr. Rowland, however. I owe him at least a taste of the suffering he would have caused me."

Rebecca shivered, and Penelope moved to stand closer to her twin. Halifax turned on his heel and slammed the door behind him as he left. They heard him turn the key and clung to one another's hands.

"I am so sorry I dragged you into such danger," Rebecca told her twin when they were alone.

"It is not your fault!" Penelope said stoutly. "It is Lord Halifax who has to answer for all of this. And one way or another I vow he will do so."

"Have you a plan?" Rebecca asked hopefully.

Penelope had to admit that she did not. "But perhaps Mr. Rowland will rescue us?" she suggested.

Rebecca shook her head. "I wish it might be so," she countered, "but I do not think it wise to count on him to do so. I think it would be far wiser if we tried to rescue ourselves."

She looked out the window and shuddered at the long drop to the ground. Escape would not be easy that way, even if they could manage to pry the iron bars from the window itself.

Rebecca looked at her twin and asked, "Well, Penelope, what do you have in your reticule?"

As Rebecca had expected, the contents of Penelope's reticule were far more interesting than her own. Rebecca carried what any young lady might carry. Penelope carried what any young woman fascinated with odds and ends and bits of nature might discover during a day's events.

Most important of all, Penelope's reticule contained a long, thin tool made of steel.

"What is that?" Rebecca asked, picking up the thing.

Penelope shrugged. "I don't know. I saw Hugh drop it and I picked it up. I meant to return it to him, but never had the chance. I've no notion what it might be for, but I think we might be able to use it to unlock the door, don't you?"

Rebecca grinned at her twin. "If we can't," she said, "Barbara will never forgive us! After all, she showed us often enough how to open doors when we had those dreadful governesses who used to lock us in. We used to be very good at it then."

Penelope used the tool, since she was the one who had found it. And she was quite correct, it was very useful, and in moments she had the door unlocked. Then, with a peek through the keyhole first, they opened the door.

They were at the end of a long corridor and fortunately the silence had accurately foretold that no one was here. The two girls looked at one another in surprise.

"Why do you suppose he left no one to guard us?" Rebecca asked.

Penelope snorted. "No doubt he thought us mere helpless females and therefore not worth having to waste men to guard." She paused and smiled a hard, cold smile. "I shall enjoy proving him wrong," she said.

"Yes, but I am still surprised he did not leave anyone in case we tried to cause trouble or needed anything," Rebecca persisted. "I think it might be wise to shut the door and move quickly, and be ready to pop into one of these doors along the way in case there is a guard and he has just stepped away for a moment or two."

Penelope did not waste time but nodded and began to creep along the corridor.

They must have made, Rebecca thought, a remarkably foolish sight as they made their way along. But neither she nor her twin wished to be caught unawares. They took turns stopping at each door in turn and listening for voices or other sounds.

These precautions proved their worth when they were scarcely halfway to the corner of the hallway. Footsteps sounded heavily from that direction and the two girls immediately darted back into the doorway they had just passed. The room was indeed deserted.

Fortunately the door did not squeak and they had it closed well in time. The room was large and all the furnishings had Holland covers over them. The heavy draperies were dusty and closed. Rebecca and Penelope headed straight for them.

Just as they whisked themselves behind the heavy folds of cloth, voices passed in the hallway outside the room. The twins looked at one another and immediately inspected the windows and how high the drop was to the ground from this side of the house.

It was a long way down, but fortunately there was a balcony outside the windows of this room. The girls stepped outside and silently closed the windows behind them.

"It may take a while for them to discover we are gone," Rebecca said thoughtfully, "but we ought not to count upon it. Someone may decide to take pity and feed us or simply check on us at any moment."

Penelope nodded her agreement even as she inspected the side of the house for a vine or pipes or anything else that might be used for escape.

"A pity there are no trees close at hand," she observed.

"Not close to this balcony," Rebecca agreed, "but if we

can manage to make our way from one balcony to another, that tree over there might do."

Penelope looked at the tree her sister was pointing at. She also gauged the distance between balconies. "I think we might do it," she agreed cautiously, "but we shall have to hike up our skirts."

Rebecca nodded grimly. Moments later, she climbed onto the railing. It was a near thing, but she made the leap safely to the next balcony. Penelope followed right behind her.

Carefully they made their way from balcony to balcony, each time getting closer to the tree. More than once they had to pause and duck down below the railings to hide as Lord Halifax's men circled the house on some sort of patrol. Still, there was no alarm for their escape.

Luck held in that none of the rooms they passed were in use. Or if they were, the heavy draperies, all closed, protected the twins from detection.

Finally they reached the tree. Crouched down, Rebecca and Penelope conferred on the next stage of their plans.

"We must time the guards and see how long each circuit takes," Penelope said.

"I have already done so," Rebecca said, a trifle smugly. "We have several minutes. Surely long enough for us to reach the ground."

"Yes, but did you notice the curtains twitched on that room below? We shall have to go in the other direction to avoid being seen. Where are we to go, once we reach the ground?" Penelope countered, with a touch of smugness of her own.

"Oh."

For several more moments, long enough for the guards to come in view again, they conferred. Finally they agreed upon a clump of bushes which they trusted to be heavy enough to hide them. And then, after taking care of one or two matters, they would make their way to the set of trees near the road. If they were fortunate, they would reach it before Mr. Rowland arrived and be able to warn him off when he did. If he did.

Neither girl dared waste time worrying over the matter. Either he would come or they would hike to the nearest town and consult the authorities there. One way or another, they would escape and have the best of Lord Halifax. Before tomorrow, with luck, he would find himself back in prison and unable to hurt anyone else.

That was the plan. Unfortunately, someone discovered they were missing and shouts began to go up. The two girls looked at one another.

Rebecca swallowed hard. "He is looking for me," she said. "I shall go back in. You must continue to escape. Steal one of the horses and go for help."

"No! I cannot leave you," Penelope protested.

"It is our only hope, now that they are alerted. Go," she repeated, giving her sister a small shove. "There is no more time to argue."

With one last hug, Rebecca leaped back to the previous balcony and entered the room there. Then she moved through it to the hallway and across, where she loudly slammed a door on the other side.

Within moments, footsteps came running. Shortly after that, she stood before Halifax in a downstairs room and he glared at her maliciously while one of his men held her head back by yanking on her hair.

"Where is your sister?" he demanded.

"I don't know," Rebecca gasped. "We decided to separate, to improve our chances of escape. I think she must be long gone by now so you had better let me go and make good your own escape."

"Which means," Halifax said, setting down his glass of brandy with a distinct snap, "that she is probably still in the house. Go look for her," he ordered the two men in the room. "I shall look after this one myself."

Chapter 21

The Westcotts were in rare form. As might have been expected, Lady Westcott was prostrate on the couch, her sister, Lady Brisbane, waving smelling salts beneath her nose. Lord Westcott was regarding the family governess, Miss Tibbles, with an awful rage in his eyes and in his voice.

"I realize, Miss Tibbles," he said, biting off each word, "that you have only been with the family for a few short years. But in those few short years, an extraordinary number of strange and very unfortunate, and one might even say scandalous, circumstances have befallen members of this family. Now you are telling me that Rebecca has run off with this Rowland fellow? And dragged along her sister as well?"

This last ended on a roar. Instead of intimidating Miss Tibbles, however, it only seemed to embolden her. She drew herself up to her full height and her voice was firm and calm as ever as she said, "I have told you everything I know. If you do not like it, that is not my fault. The girls are gone and, as I took care to ascertain, Mr. Rowland departed his lodgings in his carriage shortly before the note asked Lady Rebecca to meet him in the park. I conclude," she added acidly, "that the girl has run off with him. If you have a better explanation to offer, I should be very glad to hear it."

Lord Westcott ignored this and returned to his grievance

against the governess. "It is your fault we brought both girls to London," he replied, his color rising.

Miss Tibbles eyed him squarely. "Sooner or later you must have done so."

"You condoned bringing Mr. Rowland into the house," the earl persisted, determined to bring to her some understanding of the full measure of her sins.

"You thought the reasoning impeccable at the time," she countered.

"It was your duty to make certain my daughters were not engaged in clandestine correspondence!" he roared. "And that they did not go outside the house for secret assignations in the park, much less to take part in an elopement. It is all your fault, Miss Tibbles!"

"Nonsense." Miss Tibbles adjusted her spectacles. She did not really need them, but she had learned early on that they gave her an air of authority which helped make up for her lack of inches. "You are merely concerned for your daughters' safety. As am I. Instead of railing at one another, we should be trying to discover what next we should do to find them. I have already sent servants around to ask at the posting stations and along the north road."

Just then there was an urgent rapping at the front door. It was ignored by all and sundry, but they could not ignore the note brought upstairs a moment later.

"Sir Parker?" Lady Westcott echoed the name faintly when her husband read the note aloud.

"Must we see him now?" Lady Brisbane asked impatiently.

"Since he is one of the few men who seems to know Mr. Rowland and since Mr. Rowland appears to be involved, then yes I think we must," Lord Westcott snapped back. "He vouched for the fellow. Perhaps he can tell us where Rowland is most likely to have gone with Rebecca and Penelope."

The Earl of Westcott then told the footman to go down and fetch Sir Parker up to them.

Moments later, that gentleman walked into the drawing room and instantly grasped the situation. It was not difficult when two ladies and one gentleman were shouting at him that his friend, Mr. Rowland, was a fiend, a seducer of young women, an irredeemable rogue.

Sir Parker closed his eyes and resisted the temptation to turn tail and run. He had never been, however, a coward, and so he stood his ground.

"Mr. Rowland has not run off with your daughters," he said.

Sir Parker ignored the note thrust under his nose and waited as Lord Westcott thundered, "If Mr. Rowland has not taken off with Rebecca and Penelope, then where the devil are they? And where is he?"

"To the best of my knowledge, he is headed due west of here," Sir Parker replied calmly, "following a blue and yellow coach carrying Lord Halifax and both your daughters and however many men it may have taken to subdue them."

These words had the result of draining the color from every face in the room, including Miss Tibbles's. Indeed, Lady Westcott was so stunned, she sat bolt upright and actually forgot to moan.

"Where are they going and what, do you believe, is Lord Halifax's purpose in abducting them?" Lady Brisbane asked, her voice shaking.

Sir Parker shook his head. "I don't know. Rowland scarcely had time to send word to me. The message, of necessity, had to be brief since he was entrusting it to a street urchin. But as I understand it, he saw Halifax abduct the girls and was following the coach. I have already been to Bow Street and seen that Runners were sent on their way in pursuit. Meanwhile, I have also made my own inquiries and forwarded what information I could glean separately to Bow Street. Then I realized that perhaps I should also come here and attempt to reassure you that everything is being done to recover your daughters."

Lady Westcott so far forgot herself as to grasp Sir Parker's hand in gratitude. Lord Westcott cleared his throat and said gruffly, "Thank you for your efforts on our daughters' behalf. And thank you for coming to tell us. I, er, my apologies for suspecting Mr. Rowland of running off with our girls."

Sir Parker bobbed his head. "From the note you showed me, you had good cause to think what you did. Least said, soonest mended. And now I must be on my way. I'm off to see if I can follow the trail as well." He paused, then added, unaccustomed emotion in his own voice, "Rowland has become something like a son to me."

"I'll go with you," Westcott replied. He paused and looked at the governess. "Miss Tibbles, we may need your assistance, as well—depending on what Lord Halifax has done by the time we find the girls."

She nodded. "I shall be ready in two shakes of a lamb's tail."

And she was.

But when they reached the street and both Lord Westcott's and Sir Parker's waiting coaches, they found still another arrival just pulling up by the house. It was Lord Farrington. He leaped down from his carriage, slammed shut the door, and said to Sir Parker, "There you are! I have been trying to track you down. I've got Caldwell in the coach with me and wanted to ask what you wish me to do with him."

"Caldwell?" Lord Westcott echoed. "But I thought Rowland murdered the fellow."

"That," Sir Parker said witheringly, "is what he wished you to believe. No, he merely bundled him out of the way and allowed Halifax to believe he had murdered him."

He paused and turned to Farrington. "The devil take it, man, what took you so long bringing him back to London?"

Farrington grinned. "It seems the rather resourceful Caldwell did not wish to stay where he was put and I have spent all this time tracking him down."

"Well, you'd best take him to Bow Street and let him make a statement there," Sir Parker said.

But Farrington, despite his lack of sleep, had by now noticed the large party and its distracted nature, standing outside Lady Brisbane's townhouse.

"More games?" he asked Sir Parker.

Succinctly he was put in possession of the facts.

"I'll go along," Farrington said.

"Someone must take Caldwell to Bow Street," Sir Parker began doubtfully.

"You do so," Farrington countered. "Surely you have no wish to gallivant all over the countryside chasing after Rowland? Leave that to me."

"Very well."

The details were quickly settled and all the parties bundled into their respective coaches. And then, as if in a race, all three pulled away from the curb at a shocking pace for London.

Hugh, meanwhile, was driving as swiftly as he dared. Already he had suffered one delay when his wheel caught in a rut and the curricle almost overturned. He had knocked another coach into a ditch and been obliged to stop and offer assistance to the rattled occupants. What with apologies and all, it had been some time before he managed to be on his way again.

But it had been time that was not entirely wasted. The occupants of the ditched coach had seen the blue and yellow coach pass by some time earlier and so he knew he was on the right road. And he had been able to extract a promise that they would speak to the authorities at the nearest town and send help after him if they could.

But still, fear for Lady Rebecca and her sister lent an urgency to Rowland's journey that nothing else could have done. He did not dare stop to take more than the briefest of breaks at inns he passed. Even then, only the thought that he was able to ask whether Halifax's coach had passed by reconciled him to the need for doing so much as that.

Finally, however, he turned down the lane he had been directed to and the moment he was certain he had found the right track, he hid his curricle in the bushes and hobbled the horses. Then, on foot, he made his way toward the house, keeping a sharp eye out for guards.

A first floor window was open and Hugh quietly climbed through even though he was well aware such a convenient opening might be part of a trap.

It was his fault that Lady Rebecca and her sister were in here and it was his duty to rescue them. He only hoped he had not arrived too late to do so.

Rebecca would have preferred to show no fear before Lord Halifax. She would have ignored him completely except that she wished to distract him from thinking about either Penelope or Hugh. At least, she did not wish him to be free to anticipate how either might try to rescue her. Instead, she began to weep profusely.

"Stop that caterwauling!" he exclaimed, hurling his empty brandy glass into the fireplace.

"I can't help it," Rebecca sobbed into the handkerchief she used to cover most of her face. "I cannot help fearing what you plan for me. And for Mr. Rowland."

A short, sharp laugh. "Yes, you are right to be afraid," he allowed handsomely. "Suppose I tell you; then you need not let your imagination run rampant."

She lifted her face toward him then and seemed to bravely blink back tears. "Oh, yes," she said huskily, "I pray you, do tell me."

Halifax did. In detail. More than once Rebecca thought she would be ill. But then he might have stopped talking and she wanted him to go on talking. The longer he talked, the more time she had to think and the more time both Hugh and Penelope had to try to do what they must.

Still, she could not entirely suppress the shudders that came over her as Halifax dwelt on how he meant to use Rebecca to torment Hugh. It was as he was in the middle of this part of his plans that she saw a shadow by the doorway.

But Halifax had seen it too. In an instant he was behind her with a knife to her throat. She dug her elbow into his stomach and tried to whirl away.

He was not expecting such resistance. At the same moment she moved, Hugh seemed to launch himself through the air and land on Halifax. Rebecca reached for the nearest large, heavy object and moved to try to bring it down upon his lordship's head.

But the two men were rolling about so swiftly that she could not be certain she would not hit Hugh by mistake. And by the time she might have done it, it was too late. Two other men had rushed into the room and hauled Hugh away from Lord Halifax.

Breathing heavily, Halifax backed away. "You will regret that. Both of you," he said. "It will only make things more unpleasant for you in the end. Put down that vase, Lady Rebecca. I should hate to have to have one of my men use it on you. I prefer you conscious for what I intend to do."

Hugh lunged at that, but the two men held him securely. Swallowing hard, Rebecca slowly put the vase back where she had found it.

"Much better," Halifax said approvingly. "Now, shall we begin?"

Chapter 22

Down by the stables, Penelope crouched behind a row of hedges. She could see there was but one man on patrol, and he seemed tired for he kept yawning, but dare she trust that she was right?

She glanced over her shoulder at the house. It was growing late and she was growing desperate. Who knew what Lord Halifax would do to Rebecca? She must find a way to save her sister, for who knew how long it would take Mr. Rowland to arrive. And who knew if he would be of any use, anyway.

Penelope did not have a high opinion of the resourcefulness of the men she knew, though she was willing to allow Mr. Rowland might be a trifle more resourceful than most. Still she would not wager her sister's life on it. Or her own. No, resolution was what was wanted here.

Ah, now the man was settling down on a bench outside the stable and closing his eyes, his hands folded on his lap. He meant to nap, and that might give Penelope a chance.

She made her way around to the back side of the stables, careful to do so with very little noise. She slipped inside and went from stall to stall, looking to see if any of the horses could be ridden.

They were, she saw, bred to pull carriages and unlikely to welcome a rider on their backs. But Penelope had grown up in the country and, like all her sisters, adored horses. She had never met a creature she could not ride. Now she chose one she thought would be the most amenable and still swift enough to be of use.

She didn't bother to try to saddle it, for that would be fatal. Instead, Penelope moved quickly and silently about the stable, looking for anything that might be useful. She found several things, and made her preparations. Then she moved from stall to stall, unlatching the doors.

Penelope returned to the mount she had chosen and, talking softly, managed to climb onto the horse's back. The gelding wasn't happy, but he let her do so. Then, when she was all ready, she grabbed for the lantern she had lit and threw it to the back of the stable, behind the horses.

Instantly, at the smell of smoke, the horses began to kick and whinny and head for the stable door. The man outside heard the noise and smelled the smoke. He started for the stable, but ducked out of the way as the horses came racing out. In all the confusion, he scarcely saw that one carried a rider and headed down the lane toward the main road.

His concern was to try to put out the fire. Even as he reached for a bucket, he also remembered the stable bell and ran to ring it as loudly and as violently as he could.

Inside the house they heard the stable bell.

"What the devil?" Halifax exclaimed.

"Coming from down by the stables, it is," one of his men said, recognizing the sound. "Must be somefing wrong, the way some'un's ringing it."

"Well, give me your pistols and then go and do something about it!" Halifax exclaimed.

The men hastened to obey. That left Lord Halifax, Hugh, and Rebecca alone together. But the pistols Halifax held, one in each hand, kept him firmly in control.

"How nice and cozy," he said, showing his teeth. "A pity they were called away, but that does not mean we cannot continue as we were. Lady Rebecca, come over here!"

She did not move and after a moment, Halifax leveled

one pistol directly at Hugh. "Over here, I said," he repeated, "by the count of three, or I shoot Rowland."

Rebecca came. Halifax set one pistol down on the desk behind him and with that arm, pulled her close to his side. His fingers slid upward, reaching for her breasts.

Hugh took a step forward and Halifax cocked the pistol. "Do try it," he invited cordially. "Then I shall be able to shoot you. First one knee and then the other and then the arms and so forth. It should take you some time to die, and in great pain."

Rebecca shivered. With her eyes she begged Hugh not to move. He froze where he was. She could read the frustration in his eyes, the anger, the growing desperation.

She turned in Halifax's grasp and ran a finger up his arm to the shoulder. In a breathy, admiring voice she said, "Why Lord Halifax, I had no idea you were so masterful!"

He started, then gripped her more tightly. "Playing games, Lady Rebecca?"

"Oh, no, I wouldn't dare. Not when you have that pistol. Not when you could overpower me without a thought. Oh, Lord Halifax, you are just the man I have always been dreaming of, all my life!"

And with those final words, Rebecca threw herself against his chest, forcing him to grasp her with both arms to keep from being over thrown.

He scarcely knew what happened to him. But he knew he must act before Rowland could cross the room.

Halifax fired his pistol, hoping to scare him off. But as he did so, Rebecca flung up her arm in protest and the shot grazed her. She cried out at the sudden pain.

Halifax hastily tried to release her and flail behind him for the other pistol. Even in her pain, and with her arm bleeding, Rebecca was quicker. She grabbed it and backed away. Into Rowland's waiting arms. Still she kept the pistol leveled on Halifax.

"You miscalculated, my lord," she said to Halifax, a tiny catch in her voice as she handed the pistol to Hugh.

"My men will be back at any moment," Halifax warned Hugh. "And then you will regret everything! Both of you. Let me go and you can tend to her."

It was a tempting notion. Hugh wanted desperately to discover how badly Rebecca had been hurt. But he knew Halifax too well. If he let the man go free, then neither of them would ever be safe again.

"I shall be fine," Rebecca said quickly.

Hugh gave her a warm smile. "Can you walk?" he asked.

She nodded. "I must. I do not think we dare risk remaining here until his men return."

"You have the most unfeminine foresight," Halifax snapped at her bitterly.

"So she does," Hugh agreed fondly. "Now, shall we go?" Rebecca nodded and he went on, "Come along, Halifax. We're going for a walk."

The man blanched. "No, I won't go," he said querulously. "How do I know you don't mean to take me outside and shoot me there?"

"Because," Hugh answered, in a silkily dangerous voice, "I mean to shoot you right here unless you do precisely as I say. And I say, as soon as I have bound up Lady Rebecca's wound, we are going for a walk."

Halifax wanted to refuse. There could be no mistaking that. But in the end he was too much a coward to do so. That or he could too clearly read Hugh's willingness to shoot and he told himself that at least if he were still alive, there was a chance.

It only took moments for Hugh to tear his shirt and form a pad to place over the wound. He bound it there with his handkerchief. All the while, Rebecca held the pistol leveled steadily at Lord Halifax.

"You are," his lordship told her, his voice dripping with venom, "a most unnatural creature."

"Thank you, my lord," she said.

When he was done, Hugh took back the pistol. And then the three of them, with Halifax forced into the lead, left the room and soon the house. Hugh clasped the pistol in one hand, and his other arm supported Rebecca. He was worried about her, but he thought the bullet had only grazed her arm. It had already almost stopped bleeding. And he knew their lives might depend on putting as much distance between themselves and Lord Halifax's men as possible.

The stables were at the back of the house, so Hugh directed them toward the front. He made them move quickly, heading for a clump of trees near the lane that led to the main road. One way or another, he would get Rebecca to safety. With luck, his curricle would still be waiting. If not, he would carry her to the nearest town, if need be.

Penelope scandalized the inhabitants of the small village nearest the estate. At least she would have had they had time to consider what they were seeing. As it was, she slid off the horse the moment she reached the center of town and gasped out her need for a constable.

It took her several minutes to persuade them she meant just what she said. But soon a group of men was heading off in the direction of the estate she had just escaped from, in every sort of vehicle imaginable.

After wrestling with his conscience, for he had seen Penelope's arrival and he could not approve of a hoyden who rode bareback and with her skirts hitched high enough to allow her to do so astride, the local vicar took Penelope up in his carriage and they followed the other men.

The vicar was not altogether certain he believed Penelope's story, but whether she was mad or merely a madcap, it was clearly his duty to take her in charge and look out for her welfare.

By this time, Penelope was too grateful to have found help to cavil at the form it took. All her concern was saved for the question of whether they would be in time to rescue Rebecca and Mr. Rowland. As the large group turned into the lane and headed for the manor house, they were startled to be met by three figures trudging along the lane, one of them with pistol in hand.

As everyone drew up short, Penelope leapt down from the carriage, ignoring the exclamation of dismay from the vicar behind her, and ran to her sister.

"Rebecca! Dear heaven, you are hurt!"

" 'Ere now, miss! Which one is the villain wot you told us about?"

Penelope turned and pointed out Halifax.

"Well, then, why does the other fellow have the pistol?" someone asked reasonably.

"Because," Rowland said, grinning, "I was a trifle faster and a trifle more desperate. I managed to take the pistol from him and then I forced him to come with us."

Lady Rebecca gaped at him and then said, "And I suppose you will say I had no hand in helping you do so?"

Penelope watched, bemused, as Rowland regarded her sister meekly and said, with a perfectly straight face, "I was only trying to shield your reputation, my dear. I didn't wish these gentlemen to realize how unfeminine and unnatural you are in your foresight."

At this point Lord Halifax appeared to have reached his limit. "Can we please get on with the business of arresting me?" he demanded. "I am tired and my feet are sore from walking. There is an inn nearby that ought to do for refreshments. Surely, gentlemen, you would not begrudge me that?"

Apparently they did not. Still, Halifax's men had to be caught and the stable fire put out. It didn't take very long.

Part of the party surged on ahead, to the stable area, and soon returned with Halifax's men. Meanwhile, Hugh found his curricle and horses. It was somewhat the worse for wear, for Hugh had ignored a loosening wheel in his haste to get here, and now the thing was a trifle unsteady. It would have been wisest to wait for someone to fix it before driving the thing. But every vehicle was needed to transport the prisoners and their hastily deputized guards to the nearby inn, to where everyone agreed it was time to adjourn.

Reluctantly, Hugh handed Rebecca and Penelope up into the vicar's carriage. "For I will not risk you in mine," he said.

That poor gentleman mopped his brow at the sight of another female in such improper circumstances. Worse, this one was bleeding! Matters, he thought grimly, had gotten very much out of hand.

Even after she was settled, Hugh regarded Rebecca anxiously. "Are you certain you are all right?" he demanded. "I am the veriest beast to have pressed you so!"

She gave him another wintry smile. "You were bent on saving my life, sir, and I will not allow you to apologize for doing so! Indeed, I am most grateful."

Hugh looked up at the vicar. "Take care of her, will you?" he asked, with a wry smile. "It may not be easy, but I shall follow as quickly as I can, with the others. I dare not risk her in my curricle in the state it is in."

Even the vicar, who counted himself a very stern man, was no proof against those deep blue eyes. He found himself smiling in return and promising he would.

Chapter 23

Perhaps it was inevitable that they all, from Hugh and Halifax to Farrington and Westcott, ended up at the same inn. It was, after all, on the road from London, and the nearest to the house where Halifax had taken the girls.

But somehow it seemed an odd trick of fate that they should all have entered the main parlor at close to the same moment. It was difficult to say who was the most distressed. Or the most relieved.

Rebecca and Penelope threw themselves into Lord Westcott's arms. "Oh, Papa, we were afraid we would never see you or Mama again!"

"Good God, Rebecca! You are bleeding!"

"The merest scratch, Papa."

"Who did it?"

"Lord Halifax."

Miss Tibbles advanced upon Halifax then, and began to scold him roundly. "How dare you, sir? Your actions were not those of a gentleman! To lure my poor girl into, as she thought, a secret meeting. and then to kidnap her, yes, kidnap her and bring her all the way out here! And then to shoot her! You ought to be heartily ashamed of yourself, Lord Halifax, even if it is not my place to be telling you so."

But this was too much for the earl. "Out of my way, Miss Tibbles. I've a word or two to say to Halifax myself," Westcott said grimly, pulling off his coat and rolling up his sleeves as he advanced upon the fellow.

From next to the doorway, where they both still stood, Farrington grinned at Hugh and said, "Good work. You managed to stop and get word to Sir Parker and still get here in time to rescue Lady Rebecca and Lady Penelope. You know, of course, that the Westcotts thought you had eloped with Lady Rebecca? Sir Parker had managed to straighten out that misunderstanding by the time I got there. Oh, and by the by, Caldwell is in London, at Bow Street, right now."

"What took so long?" Hugh asked, keeping an anxious eye on Rebecca.

"He'd slipped away from where I left him. It took me forever to track him down and I finally found him preparing to take ship from England. You ought to have seen his face when he realized he was overtaken."

Hugh clapped a hand around Farrington's shoulder and said, "Come have a drink and tell me all about it."

Meanwhile, the local constable and his hastily assembled group of helpers looked utterly bewildered by the whole situation. Still, they grimly kept a close grip on their captives. Until, that is, two rather rough looking individuals came up to the constable and introduced themselves as Bow Street Runners.

"We'll take charge of the prisoners now," one of them told the constable firmly.

"Aye, they'll be looking for 'is lordship in London, they will," the second chimed in.

The constable was only too happy to comply.

The vicar kept shaking his head and muttering comments to himself as to the ways of the wicked, but no one asked him to explain what he meant.

Eventually Lord Westcott was satisfied and, glaring down at Lord Halifax, who now had a blackened left eye to match the right, began to roll his sleeves back down. Then he went in search of Hugh.

"I understand I owe my daughters' safety to you, sir. My heartfelt thanks," he said gruffly, when he found him.

Hugh took the hand held out to him. "I could do no less," he replied. Then, with a sidelong glance at the uproar going on all around them, he added, "I wonder, could we, do you think, talk for a moment privately over there?"

Westcott agreed. He had a good notion what it was Mr. Rowland wished to say to him, and at the moment he was inclined to hear the fellow out and reply quite favorably.

Rebecca would have tried to follow her father and Hugh, but having rung a peal over Lord Halifax's head, and stood transfixed by the sight of the Earl of Westcott engaged in fisticuffs, Miss Tibbles now turned her minatory gleam upon the girls. It was a sufficiently daunting gleam that both Rebecca and Penelope found themselves backing up as she advanced toward them.

"What, precisely, were you thinking, Rebecca?" Miss Tibbles demanded. "To be indulging in a clandestine correspondence would be bad enough, but to agree to a secret assignation and to drag your sister along into the face of danger, well it is quite the outside of enough! And you, Penelope, how could you be so foolish as to agree?"

Her back against the wall, Rebecca tried to explain. "I did not know I was taking Penelope into danger. If I had, I would most certainly not have gone myself."

"You could not expect me to allow Rebecca to go on her own," Penelope chimed in. "And it did sound harmless, truly it did."

Miss Tibbles sniffed. "That is neither here nor there. Even had there been no danger, even had the note really come from Mr. Rowland, you ought not to have gone. Why, if anyone knew what Rebecca was doing, it would have sunk her beneath reproach entirely."

Rebecca tried to coax Miss Tibbles into a better mood.

"No one was supposed to see us," she said. "It was morning. No one was supposed to be about. I thought that was why the time was set as it was."

"Except that it was not your Mr. Rowland, but rather Lord Halifax who was planning to meet you," Miss Tibbles said sternly. "Really, Rebecca, it was unpardonably foolish of you, and I thought I was never going to see the two of you girls again!"

And then, to the utter surprise and consternation of both girls, Miss Tibbles burst into tears and hugged them both. They looked at one another, helpless to know what to say to this side of the woman they had never seen before.

Lord Halifax, meanwhile, feeling most abused, made several unsuccessful attempts to bribe the Bow Street Runners. That is to say, they were perfectly willing to take his money but not in the least willing to let him go.

Then he tried to implicate Hugh in his troubles. "He killed Philip Caldwell, you know," Lord Halifax told the Runners. "Murdered him without a trace of remorse. I've a man who saw it all!"

The Runners were not impressed. "Why won't anyone believe me? I've said it more than once and nothing is done," Halifax demanded.

Rowland, who had finished his conversation with Lord Westcott in time to overhear this charge, now strolled over to the Runners. He even patted Halifax on the shoulder kindly.

"Did no one tell you?" he asked solicitously. "It was all a ruse. Bow Street has known it from the moment of your arrest. That is why no one has tried to arrest me."

Farrington, who had followed Hugh over, now said with a grin, "At this very moment, Philip Caldwell is cooling his heels in Bow Street. Not a hair harmed on his head."

Halifax's henchmen, seeing which way the wind was blowing, suddenly became quite eager to tell everything they knew. The two Bow Street Runners could not write things down in their notebooks fast enough.

Eventually, a great deal later, Rebecca somehow found herself alone in a private parlor with Mr. Rowland. Her arm had been looked at and bound up again by Miss Tibbles and a local surgeon. She had been given a restorative cordial and fed a light tea. At some point, however, everyone had disappeared. Except Hugh.

He advanced upon her and she looked down at her hands. She felt, to her astonishment, suddenly, unaccountably shy.

Hugh promptly grasped both her hands in his own and raised first one palm and then the other to his lips as he kissed each one. Then he pulled her to her feet. As he did so, he kept his eyes firmly fixed upon her face.

"Mr. Rowland," Rebecca protested nervously, "I do not think this is proper, and Papa may walk in at any moment. Or Miss Tibbles."

"No they won't," Hugh said promptly, as he removed her bonnet.

"They won't?" Rebecca asked warily as Hugh bent forward and pressed a kiss at the base of her neck.

She shivered. Perhaps it was a good thing she was not wearing a hat.

"No, they won't," Hugh agreed. "I spoke to your father before I came in here," he added, kissing first one eyelid and then the other, "and he assured me he would prevent Miss Tibbles from breaking in on us."

"Oh? And why did Papa say he would do so?" Rebecca asked, oddly breathless.

"He said he would do so," Hugh replied, kissing first one corner and then the other of her mouth, "because I asked him for your hand in marriage. He said he was perfectly willing to give it to me, and the sooner the better. He was very nice about the whole thing."

To his consternation, she giggled. Hugh leaned back with a frown of confusion.

Rebecca promptly explained. "I can far more easily picture Papa telling you that you can marry me and be damned than that he spoke in such polite terms, given the provocation he has endured this day."

Hugh grinned. "Well, perhaps your terms are a trifle closer to the words he used than mine, but the important thing is, he is willing to consent to our marriage. What I should like to know is whether you will consent as well."

But this was too much for Rebecca. She pushed Hugh away, and then glared at him. She planted her hands on her hips, ignoring the throbbing sensation in her arm.

"Well, I like that!" she said with some asperity. "I have been telling you and telling you that we ought to be married, and now you act as though you aren't certain I shall agree? And as though it is quite your own idea?"

He looked at her meekly. "Does that mean you do agree?" he asked.

"Why?" she demanded.

"Why, what?" he echoed, taken aback.

"Why do you suddenly wish to marry me?" Rebecca demanded.

"Your eloquence persuaded me?" he suggested meekly.

She glared at him and tapped her foot. He tried again.

"Caldwell has been found and I no longer live under the cloud of having everyone suspect I did away with him?"

She snorted in disbelief.

"I was certain I was about to lose you and couldn't bear the thought?"

He meant it. There was no doubt. His eyes, his face, the way he reached for her, all bore evidence of his sincerity, and Rebecca was not proof against it. He seemed to know she had begun to waver.

"When you were shot, I knew I could not, would not want to live without you." Then, his lips twitching mischievously, with a look of wide-eyed innocence on his face, he asked, coaxingly, "Please, Lady Rebecca, will you marry me? I know I shall need rescuing, every so often, and I cannot think of anyone I should rather have rescue me."

She tried to continue to look severe, but first one corner of her mouth and then the other twitched upward. Still, she was not entirely convinced.

"What about Felicity Hamilton?" she asked.

Hugh sunk his head in his hands. "Am I never to forget my sins?" he demanded.

"That depends upon what sort of sins they were," Rebecca replied reasonably.

He sighed. "I loved Felicity Hamilton. Desperately. And when her father said she could marry me, I was in alt. Unfortunately, the more she grew to know me, the more she came to dislike the man I was. I was not fashionable enough or possessed of the social graces she adored. She called me arrogant and a tyrant, and I was. I fear I fell sadly short of the bridegroom she envisioned and, in the end, she wisely called it off."

His voice grew more and more grim as he spoke until his eyes held a bleakness that tugged at Rebecca's heartstrings. "So you see," he concluded, "I am a very poor bargain. Perhaps you'd best turn me down after all. Except that I do not think I will know how to go on living if you do."

Rebecca reached out and took his face between her hands. "You foolish wretch!" she said softly. "Felicity Hamilton was a silly goose, too want-witted to know how to value you. I am not, I assure you, such an idiot. I shall adore you until the day I die."

His eyes lit up with warmth, with hope, with something smoldering that was older than time. He could not resist adding, "It is not only Felicity but my mother and father and brother who agreed I was not fit for polite company."

"Well I am glad you told me so," Rebecca said warmly,

"for now I know that I do not wish to meet any of them. Not if they abuse you so shamefully!"

"Does this mean you will marry me?" Hugh asked, hopefully.

Rebecca tried to make him wait, but she could not. She threw her arms around his neck and whispered into his ear, "Yes, oh, yes, Hugh, I most certainly will!"

He was not entirely correct, however, in having said Miss Tibbles would not intrude. She chose precisely that moment to open the parlor door.

At the sight of the entwined couple she hastily whisked inside the parlor and shut the door behind herself. "That is quite enough of that!" she said severely. "The coaches are waiting and it is past time that we were on our way back to London. Your mother and aunt will be waiting for word of your safety, and your sister's, Rebecca."

Then Miss Tibbles paused, stared at the entwined couple, and added in acid tones, "Do you not think it would be best for the both of you if we were to be able to return to London some time this evening? I have no doubt Mr. Rowland has just come up to scratch. And that you, Rebecca, have accepted him. Nothing else could justify such behavior as I now see. But I should like to minimize the harm that could be done if word should get out of this latest escapade of yours."

"But Miss Tibbles," Rebecca said innocently, "Mr. Rowland and I intend to live in the north, anyway. It can scarcely matter there what the tattle-mongers say in London."

Hugh stared at her in surprise. "Where," he said carefully, "did you get the notion that we will be living in the north?"

It was Rebecca's turn to look at him in astonishment. "Is that not where your estates are?"

He nodded.

"Well, then where else would I wish to live?" she asked with some exasperation.

"London, perhaps?" he suggested.

"Now what gave you such a bird-witted notion as that?" Rebecca demanded. "Have I ever said I wished to live in London?"

"Well, no," he admitted, rubbing the side of his nose. "I simply assumed you would wish to be close to your family and to the social life of the *ton*. Don't you?"

"I can see," Rebecca said with no little exasperation, "that you have a great deal to learn about me. And about marriage. I warn you now, Mr. Rowland, that it is not wise to make assumptions. I should advise you always to ask what I wish, rather than presume you know."

He grinned at her. "I shall endeavor to remember that," he said with mock meekness.

From the doorway, Miss Tibbles spoke in more acid tones than before. "This is all very pretty, but the others are waiting. It is time to go!"

Rebecca and Hugh looked at one another. He helped her to smooth out her skirts and settled her bonnet neatly on her head. Then he offered her his arm and with chins tilted high, the couple swept past Miss Tibbles and out the door.

Miss Tibbles snorted loudly, but she followed. And if she smiled a rather tender smile behind their backs, well, it was one she knew they could not see.

Epilogue

Hugh softly stroked the side of his wife's cheek, hoping to wake her. He had some very pleasant notions as to what they could do once she did. The staff, after all, was well trained and had strict orders they were never to disturb the master and mistress until they rang for their morning tea.

Outside, cold winds blew and winter rain rattled the windowpanes, but inside, in this bed, Hugh felt heat rising through him. It was still a matter of wonder and awe to Hugh that Rebecca was his wife. He stroked her cheek again.

Rebecca murmured appreciatively and shifted in her sleep until she pressed along the length of him. But to Hugh's disappointment, she did not wake up.

Hugh tried again. This time he blew into her ear and when that did not work, nibbled on the earlobe. It was, he thought, one of her favorite things for him to do. And he wanted her to wake in a very happy, contented mood.

But Rebecca still did not wake up.

With a sigh, Hugh rolled onto his back and put his arms behind his head. He was a patient man, he told himself. He could wait until she awoke.

The next thing he knew, Rebecca had thrown herself onto his chest and kissed him soundly. "Why on earth did you stop?" she demanded with a frown.

Automatically his arms went around her. "But I thought you were still asleep," he protested.

She gave a disgusted snort, then kissed him again. "You give up far too easily," she said.

"Well I am very sorry if you think I should be less considerate of you," he said in injured tones. "I thought perhaps you needed the sleep."

Rebecca raised herself up on her elbows. "I thought we had a discussion, indeed I know we have had more than one discussion, on the subject of your assuming you know what I wish. I am getting very tired of it."

"Yes, my love," he said meekly.

She was not deceived. Rebecca sighed and lowered herself to his chest again. His lovely, warm chest.

"What I need," she said in a husky whisper as she gently stroked his cheek, "is to be well and truly loved by a very eager husband this morning."

Hugh grinned and promptly proved himself quite happy to oblige her.

Some hours later, they sat together in the drawing room. Rebecca was knitting garments for the child they had just learned would soon be entering their lives. She stopped, occasionally, to feel her stomach, still astonished at the miracle that was taking place inside. She could not believe happiness could be so full.

And then a caller was announced. Both Rebecca and Hugh were on their feet before he even set foot in the room.

"Sir Parker! How wonderful to see you."

"Come in, sir. Come over by the fire and warm yourself. What brings you here?"

There was more than a hint of apprehension in Rebecca's mind as she waited for his answer. Had he come to take Hugh away for another mission? She knew that what he had once done had mattered greatly. She also knew she could not bear to have him risk his life like that ever again. Sir Parker took a maddening length of time to come to the point.

"What a pleasant domestic scene," he said.

"We are happy here," Hugh agreed.

"I understand you are starting a school. For London urchins to be raised out here in the fresh air and sunshine," Sir Parker said.

"And for local children as well. Those whose parents have been killed in the mills," Rebecca added, drawing closer to Hugh.

He put an arm around her and kissed the top of her head. "My wife cannot bear to see any creature in need without trying to help," he said affectionately.

Sir Parker grinned. "And the joining of your two fortunes certainly makes it possible."

"What about you?" Hugh asked delicately. "What are you doing these days? Still up to the same tricks?"

To Rebecca's astonishment, he blushed a fiery red, even as he shook his head. "No, m'boy," he said, "I've taken a page from your book. I'm about to retire."

Rebecca felt a wave of relief go through her. "Indeed, sir? And what do you mean to do?" she asked, more amiable now that she knew Hugh was not at risk.

Sir Parker looked at her and his eyes twinkled as though he knew precisely what her thoughts and fears had been. Still, it took him some moments to come to the point. He colored, he coughed, he cleared his throat.

Finally he said, "I've taken another page from Rowland's book. I've gotten married."

"Married?"

"That's wonderful, sir. Who is the fortunate lady?"

Again Sir Parker blushed a fiery red. "Well, er, that is to say, oh, the devil take it, I've gone and wed Lady Tarren these two days past!"

"Lady Tarren?" Rebecca and Hugh echoed together in stunned accents.

"Yes, and you needn't tell me it will turn the *ton* on its head, for I know it perfectly well," Sir Parker said, instantly defensive. "And the devil's own time I had, getting her to agree. Afraid she would drag me down, or some such rot! But I know her worth, even if she and the rest of the world do not. She is the lady, Rowland, who helped us so much in the case you were on."

"I'll be damned," Hugh said, and then he started to laugh.

"What is so funny, dearest?" Rebecca asked warily.

"Yes," Sir Parker said dryly, "what is so amusing?"

"I was just thinking how many eyebrows we will raise when we all appear in London together," Hugh said with a mischievous grin.

Sir Parker looked startled. "I hadn't meant to ask you to receive her."

"No?" Rebecca demanded, advancing on the poor fellow. "And just what did you expect us to do? Cut her? Cut the both of you? Oh, no, you and she will both be guests in our house, Sir Parker. And at any ball we give."

Sir Parker looked positively stunned now, sending Hugh off into fresh gales of laughter. "Give it over, sir. My dear wife will not rest until she has rescued the pair of you as she once did me. And to tell you the truth, sir, I am very glad of it."

Slowly Sir Parker began to grin. He even managed to wink at Rebecca and say, "I knew I was right to help you get leg-shackled to the boy! But I shan't ask, or even allow, you to do any such thing. Lady Tarren and I leave for India before the week is out."

"India?" Hugh echoed, startled.

"Yes, well, it seems there are some problems to be resolved and someone thought I could be useful there," Sir Parker said diffidently. "Not officially, you understand. But perhaps with a word here or there, or my ears kept open, when need be. And my wife will be accepted more readily, for I am told the ladies there are starved for company."

Sir Parker paused and stared into the fireplace. Then he

looked back at his host and hostess. His voice was serious as he said, "I love my wife. And I don't wish to see her unhappy—as she would be here in England."

Which made Rebecca ask, "Where is Lady Tarren now?"

Sir Parker named a nearby inn. "We're on our honeymoon, you see," he told her.

Rebecca rose to her feet and advanced on him. Her eyes were like daggers as she said, "And you didn't bring her here? Go, sir, and fetch your wife!"

Sir Parker was too wise a man to argue. Within the hour, Lady Tarren was sitting in their drawing room and Hugh, his arm around Rebecca, found himself thinking he could not imagine being more happy than he was right now.

Rebecca heartily agreed.

Author's Note

With every new book in the Westcott series, I fall more and more in love with this family. I loved Hugh, and wished I could take him home myself. And I found myself worrying about Penelope and Miss Tibbles. Fortunately, each one will have her own book and I will get to tell their stories. Coming next:

Penelope believes she does not ever want to be married. To avoid it she is willing to enter into a false betrothal with a man who seems to despise marriage as much as she does. But nothing is ever quite what it seems.

As always—happy reading!